THE LAWMAN RETURNS

LYNETTE EASON

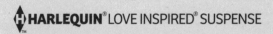

Recycling programs
for this product may
not exist in your area.

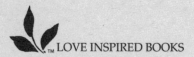 LOVE INSPIRED BOOKS

ISBN-13: 978-0-373-67635-4

THE LAWMAN RETURNS

Copyright © 2014 by Lynette Eason

www.Harlequin.com

Printed in U.S.A.

"Someone's in the house, Clay," Sabrina whispered.

Fear shooting through his veins, Clay bolted for the golf cart. "What do you mean? Where are you?"

"Hiding in the bathroom. I woke up when I heard footsteps in the hall. Hurry!"

"Stay on the line with me. I'm only a couple of minutes away. Do you know where he is now?"

"No. I can't hear anything." A thud sounded.

"Sabrina?"

"He's in the room, just outside the door. He's not making any effort to be quiet."

Clay had to strain to hear her. Her terror reached through the line and grabbed him by the throat. "I'm thirty seconds away."

Each second seemed like a lifetime until finally, the cottage came into view.

Dread pounded through him. He shoved aside his heavy coat and gripped his Glock, pulling it from the shoulder holster and holding it ready.

He stepped up onto the porch, stood to the side and twisted the knob to the front door. Unlocked. He pushed it open.

Silence greeted him. Fear clutched him. Was he too late?

Books by Lynette Eason

Love Inspired Suspense

LYNETTE EASON

makes her home in South Carolina with her husband and two children. Lynette has taught in many areas of education over the past ten years and is very happy to make the transition from teaching school to teaching at writers' conferences. She is a member of RWA (Romance Writers of America), FHL (Faith, Hope & Love) and ACFW (American Christian Fiction Writers). She is often found online and loves to talk writing with anyone who will listen. You can find her at www.facebook.com/lynette.eason or www.lynetteeason.com.

The Lord does not look at the things people look at.
People look at the outward appearance,
but the Lord looks at the heart.
—*1 Samuel* 16:7

Dedicated to the heroes who put their lives
on the line every day. To those in social work
and law enforcement, thank you for what you do.
And of course, as always, this book is dedicated to
my Lord and Savior who allows me to chase my
dream and draw others to Him while doing it.

ONE

Social worker Sabrina Mayfield pressed the phone to her ear as she pushed away from her desk. "Jordan? What is it?"

"I need your help," he whispered. "I think I'm in trouble."

"What kind of trouble?"

Jordan Zellis, one of her kids who'd been in the system but was trying to make something of himself, would call only if he truly needed help.

"I...I need a ride. Will you come get me?"

Sabrina tightened her grip on the phone. "Have you been drinking?"

"No, j-just hanging out with friends. I...ah... started taking some pictures of...you know...the trees and birds and stuff and they...ah...left me here."

"Where?"

He gave her the address. She heard shuffling and a whisper. Then silence. "Jordan?"

"I'm here."

Her worry spiked at the new tone in his voice. "What is it?"

"Never mind. I can get home. I'm fine. Don't come here. Just…just don't come here, okay?"

"Jordan Zellis, what's going on? You tell me right now." Sabrina hoped the maternal-sounding order would get him to talk.

Silence. Sabrina wondered if she'd pushed too hard. Then she heard him suck in a deep breath. "Oh, boy. I think I may be in some deep trouble. I just now found something. I didn't know…" His voice shook.

"Found what, Jordan?"

An audible gulp. "I think I might know who killed Steven Starke."

Her throat tightened. Steven Starke, her friend and book buddy. And a Wrangler's Corner deputy who'd been found dead almost four weeks ago. "What? Who? Who killed him?"

"Don't come here," Jordan whispered. "It's dangerous."

"Which is why you shouldn't be there. Get out now."

"I can't leave. I've got to get— Uh-oh—"

"Jordan?"

But he was gone, the line disconnected.

Sabrina punched in the number for the police department and raced to her car, calling over her shoulder to her boss that she'd be back soon.

"Jordan's in trouble. I'm going to find out what's going on."

Rachel came to her door. "You be careful."

Sabrina waved and pushed through the glass doors, her heart pounding. She gave the information to Tara, the dispatcher, who promised she'd have someone on the way. "Sabrina, don't do anything stupid."

"When have I ever done anything stupid?"

Tara paused. "Well, true, I can't think of anything, but there's always a first time."

Sabrina silently agreed. She knew she'd beat the police there. She was only a little over two miles from the address Jordan had given her, but he'd sounded so scared on the phone. He needed her.

Within minutes, she pulled into the gravel drive and stopped to stare at the rusted, dilapidated trailer.

Mondays never brought anything good, and today didn't look as if it was going to be the exception.

She couldn't help wondering if she went in, would she come out in one piece.

Wrangler's Corner, Tennessee, population 1,037, had its share of beauty—and problems, depending on which side of the mountain one lived on. The most prevalent issues in the small town were unemployment and abject poverty.

Dark blankets covered the windows on the inside

of the trailer, and trash littered the outside. Someone had strung a sad little strand of Christmas lights around the door of the trailer as though to attempt to offer a small ray of hope.

It didn't work.

Swallowing her nerves, Sabrina opened the car door, stepped out and tugged her fleece pullover down around her hips. She ignored the late-November wind that whipped her hair across her eyes and sent a chill up her spine.

She approached the ragged wood meant to pass as the front porch. At the bottom of the steps, she assessed it. Would it hold her? She placed one foot on the first step, then the second. It trembled but held.

She reached the top and banged on the door. "Jordan? Are you in there?" Nothing but the sound of the dog barking next door. "Come on, Jordan, you called me!"

The teen had been on her radar for a while. She'd done everything she could to help the kid, even trying to foster his interest in photography and meeting him at the office to tutor him after school. It seemed as if he'd been trying so hard lately, going to school and not causing any trouble. Until now.

Although she had to admit, he'd sounded truly scared on the phone. She banged on the door again. "Jordan!"

A thump sounded from inside. She jerked and

stepped back. What was she doing? She shivered. He'd warned her not to come, that it was dangerous. When she'd put the address in her GPS and realized where she was going, she'd almost backed out and let the police handle it.

But Jordan had sounded so scared. And Steven had been her friend. If there was a chance she could find out who killed him, she wasn't going to pass it up.

However, getting killed wouldn't help anyone. She didn't normally worry about that, but in her line of work, she never kidded herself that it couldn't happen. People got real testy when you took their kids away from them. And sometimes she had to go into areas it was best she didn't go.

At least not without backup.

She glanced back at her car, then at her watch. Where was the officer? Scanning the area, she spotted a neighbor directly across from her. The woman caught her eye, then stepped back to close the door.

People around here minded their own business. It was safer that way.

She took another step up and held on to the rickety railing. Her nose twitched. The smell of ammonia hung in the air. A hose ran the length of the trailer to disappear into a cracked window.

She knocked again. "Jordan? Come on."

A clanging sounded to her left. She jerked and

turned, slow and easy. Had one of the neighbors dropped something? Kicked a metal can?

Nothing. No, wait.... A shadow? Was someone around the corner of the trailer?

Her gaze flitted from one trailer to the next, looking for any sign of life. *Deserted* was the word that came to mind. Or everyone was in hiding.

A bad feeling gathered in her midsection, and her pulse picked up speed as her adrenaline surged.

She glanced back toward the end of the trailer where she thought she'd seen the shadow. Was someone watching her?

Ever since Steven had been murdered four weeks ago, she'd felt watched. Spied on. And right now she definitely didn't feel safe. She glanced back at her car, then swiveled to look at the trailer. But what if Jordan was in there and he needed her? What if he was hurt?

She called the Wrangler's Corner dispatch. Tara answered. "I'm at the Prescott trailer. Where's my backup, Tara?"

"He's on the way. Should be pulling in any minute."

"Tell him I'll be waiting in my car."

"Will do."

She hung up.

A low wail from inside the trailer reached her ears. She gasped. A baby crying? Or at least a young child. Or was it some sort of animal?

Oh, Lord, please tell me what to do.

She lifted her chin. Only one thing to do when no one answered the door and she thought a kid might need help.

She twisted the knob and felt her heart sink.

The door was locked.

She'd spun to head back to her car to find out where her backup was when a loud crack sounded, followed by a thud near her left ear.

Sabrina froze for a split second. Had someone just shot at her?

Sheriff's deputy Clay Starke wheeled to a stop in front of the beat-up trailer. He heard the sharp crack and saw the side of the trailer spit metal.

A shooter.

The woman on the porch careened down the steps and bolted toward him. Terror radiated from her, spiking his adrenaline. He shoved open the door to the passenger side. "Get in!"

Breathless, she landed in the passenger seat and slammed the door. Eyes wide, pupils dark black holes in the blue surrounding them, she lifted shaking hands to push her blond hair out of her eyes.

Clay got on his radio and reported shots fired at the Prescott trailer.

He glanced through the back of the squad car. If someone was shooting, they needed to be somewhere else. He cranked the car and started to back out of the drive.

She grabbed his arm. "No! We can't leave!"

"What?" He stepped on the brakes. "Lady, if someone's shooting, I'm getting you out of here."

She whirled to look out the back, then whipped around to stare at the trailer. "But I think Jordan's in there and I can't leave without him."

"Jordan?"

"A boy I work with. He called me for help. He sounded scared. I'm worried he might be hurt."

Clay put the car back in Park. "Then stay down and let me check it out."

She grabbed his arm. "But if you get out, he might shoot you."

That would definitely ruin his day, but if a kid was in trouble…

He waited. No more shots. "Stay put. I think he might be gone."

"Or waiting for one of us to get out of the car."

True. He could feel her gaze on him, studying him, dissecting him. He frowned. "What is it?"

"You."

He shot a glance behind them, then let his eyes rove the area until he'd gone in a full circle and was once again looking into her pretty face. "What about me?"

Red crept into her cheeks. "You look so much like Steven. Are you his brother?"

He stilled, focusing in on her. "I'm Clay Starke. You knew my brother?"

"Clay? I'm Sabrina Mayfield. Steven and I were good friends. He talked about you so often, I feel like I know you well."

Sabrina Mayfield. Wow. "We'll have to catch up later. Can you give me details about what's going on here?"

"One of my clients called me. He doesn't actually live here, but this is where he asked me to meet him." She met his gaze. "I don't know what he's doing here, but he said he thought he knew who killed Steven and he needed me to come get him."

Shock raced through Clay. Finally. After weeks with nothing, this could be the break he'd been looking for. "Then I want to know what he knows."

"Well, we have to find him first." She paused and looked out the window. "Without getting shot, preferably."

Clay checked in with backup. "What's your ETA?"

"Five minutes."

Clay stiffened. "Why so long? I've got a possible shooter here!"

"Car wreck on I-40. Fatalities involved. All units responded. Now I've got two heading your way as fast as they can. More coming ASAP. Sit tight and don't take any unnecessary risks."

Right. He'd heard the car-wreck call but hadn't thought about it, since he'd already had his assignment.

And there hadn't been any reports of shots when he'd gotten it. Great. He had a possible shooter and was on his own with a woman and a possible kid to protect.

"I didn't realize you were back," Sabrina said. Her voice quivered and she clasped her hands together in front of her. "Steven said you were really busy in Nashville. That you'd just passed your detective's exam." She seemed to want to talk about anything but what had happened. What might still be happening.

Her way of coping, probably.

"Yes." He forced the word from his tight throat as guilt ate at him. He should have come home when Steven called him. But he hadn't, and his brother had died. Now Clay was home to find out who'd killed him. His first week back in Wrangler's Corner he'd attended his brother's funeral. The second week had consisted of the sheriff, Ned Anderson, convincing him he needed to take the now-open deputy position. The past two weeks had been spent getting into a routine. And while his main goal was to find his brother's murderer, he'd also had to deal with ongoing family stuff.

Clay swallowed hard and pushed Steven out of his mind. For now. He craned his neck and looked through the windows, behind, in front. "No sign of the shooter."

"No one's answering the door. I think I heard a child crying." She gripped the door handle.

"Any shots from inside the trailer?"

"No, but I'm afraid for Jordan. He didn't answer the door when I knocked, but I heard...something. It was a child. I'm almost sure of it."

"Stay here."

He climbed out of the car. The trailer door opened just as he took a step. A young boy peered out. When he saw Clay, his eyes widened and he slammed the door.

The passenger door opened, and the social worker darted toward the trailer.

"Hey!"

"Sorry," she yelled over her shoulder. "That's Tony, Jordan's little brother." Before he could stop her, she was back up the steps and banging on the door.

Clay followed, expecting to hear the bark of a rifle and feel the bite of a bullet.

He leaned around her and tried the door. "Locked."

"Tony! Open the door, hon!"

He was close enough to get a whiff of a tangy orange scent that almost covered the ammonia smell. Subtle and spicy. He was also close enough to see the bullet hole in the trailer next to her head.

He made sure he had her covered but squirmed as the middle of his back tingled. A perfect target for a shooter.

A wailing cry split the air. Clay lifted a brow. "Okay, that's it." He moved around Sabrina, leaned his shoulder against the flimsy door and shoved. Hard.

With a pop, the door swung in. Clay stepped inside and came to a stop. In the space of about half a second, he noticed two things. The stench that turned his stomach—and two pairs of bright blue eyes that met his. Two children stood at the entrance to the hallway, looking as if they were ready to bolt.

The little girl wrapped her arms around her big brother and buried her face in his stomach, but not before Clay saw the tears on her cheeks, heard her trying to stifle her sobs.

The big brother settled his hands on her shoulders and glared back at Clay, defiance and fear mingling.

Sabrina stepped around him. "Tony? Maria? What are you guys doing here?" Her voice was soft and low. Clay decided if he was a kid, he would have trusted her instantly. "Where's Jordan?"

"He left," Tony said.

"Why would he leave you here?"

The boy shrugged, trying to be brave and failing miserably. "He looked out the window and said for us to sneak away as soon as he was out of sight. He said to be careful 'cause there was a bad man outside. He said he'd make sure the bad man followed him while we got away and hid in the woods. Then he'd come back and take us home."

"Bad man?" Clay asked.

"I saw you when I opened the door. I thought you might be the bad man."

"He's a deputy, hon," Sabrina said. "Didn't you see his uniform?"

Tony's lower lip trembled, but he managed a manly shrug. "I don't know. But we weren't scared or nothin'."

Sabrina moved forward to gather the little girl in her arms and whisper in her ear.

While Sabrina talked to the children, Clay took in the surroundings. Everything around him shouted meth lab. The smell, the hose through the window, the Pyrex bowls on the stove, the blankets and plastic on the windows. He turned and spoke into his radio. "Got a possible meth lab here. We're going to need someone to clean it up."

He wondered who the sheriff would call. Federal law mandated only DEA-certified individuals could dismantle a meth lab. Clay seriously doubted there was anyone qualified in Wrangler's Corner.

He checked the window again. So Jordan had seen a "bad man" and left to draw him away from the trailer so the little ones could sneak out.

Clay touched her arm. "Come on, Sabrina, get them and let's go There's no telling what we're breathing."

Sabrina held out her hand to Tony. "Please, come with me, sweetheart."

Tony reached for her hand and then froze. His eyes widened, and fear flashed across his face.

Clay spun to find himself staring down the barrel of a Winchester .45.

TWO

Sabrina gave a small cry and threw herself in front of the children. Stan Prescott stood in the open door with his rifle leveled at Clay's head. "Stan, what are you doing?"

"You're trespassing."

"And you're going to jail," Clay said. "Unless you put that gun away. Last time I checked, shooting at people was a crime."

Stan snorted. "My whole life is a crime. What are you doing on my property? What are those kids doing here?"

"Why were you shooting at me? Where's Jordan?" Sabrina asked.

"Shooting at you? I wasn't shooting at nobody, but I'm a-fixin' to."

"Put the gun down," Clay ordered. His sharp tone bounced off Stan, who kept the weapon level and mostly steady. "Who's Jordan?"

Sabrina noted the missing teeth, the sores on his face. He and Clay were the same age, she remembered Steven saying, but Stan looked a good twenty years older. She curled her fingers into fists. She sent up silent prayers as Clay held his hands where Stan could see them.

"Why are you even arguing about this, man?" Clay asked. "Where's Lacey?"

Fury flashed. "She left me. Now, why are you in my home?" Gravel crunched outside under the wheels of the cruisers as the police arrived, completely unaware of what was going on inside the little trailer.

Stan heard it, too, and he flinched, moved inside and shut the door behind him.

Her stomach twisted. What would he do? How would they get past him?

She realized this might very well become a hostage situation. "Stan? The cops are outside. You don't want any trouble, do you?" She kept her voice low.

Stan swallowed, and the gun wavered.

Clay moved and tackled the man to the trailer floor.

Sabrina wrapped her arms around the children's shoulders and hurried them to the back bedroom. Away from the possibility of being shot if the gun went off. "Stay here," she whispered.

A small hand gripped hers. "Don't leave me," Maria begged.

Sabrina's heart slammed against her chest. What

to do? Clay might need her help. But Maria had a firm grip, and the terror in her eyes said she wasn't going to let Sabrina out of her sight.

Sabrina heard the thumps and grunts of the fight going on in the front room. Her eyes jumped from the unmade bed to the end table to the dresser as she fought to figure out what she should do to help Clay. Tony wiggled away from her, and when he did, a small black object dropped to the floor. Her eyes zoomed in on the wallet, and she drew in a deep breath. And coughed. First things first. She knelt. "I've got to, for just a minute. I need to help Mr. Clay, okay?"

Tony pulled his sister from Sabrina. "Okay. Go help him."

Sabrina shot him a grateful look and raced down the short hall to find Clay and Stan locked together, Stan's fingers wrapped around the rifle, Clay's grip around Stan's wrist. Sabrina grabbed the nearest lamp, hefted it and brought it down across the back of Stan's shoulders.

He gave a harsh cry and went limp. The brief moment was enough for Clay to yank the rifle away. Stan staggered to his feet, lunged for the back door and crashed through it.

Sabrina bolted to the window as Clay scrambled after the man. The officers, caught by surprise, weren't ready for the wild man who'd burst from the trailer, and soon Stan disappeared into the trees.

Deputies gave chase. Clay stumbled after them but tripped and fell down the steps to land with a thud at the bottom. He turned, his face red, a welt on his cheek, puckered and sore looking. Sabrina met him at the bottom of the back porch steps, which seemed to be in much better condition than the front. "Are you all right?"

"Yes."

She whirled. "I'm going to get the kids."

"I'm going after Stan." He grunted and hauled himself to his feet.

She heard his pounding footsteps as she hurried back into the trailer to find Tony and Maria clutching one another while an officer knelt in front of them. Officer Donnie Kingston. She'd worked with him before.

Maria spotted Sabrina and broke away from her brother to hurl herself into Sabrina's arms. Stunned, Sabrina hesitated only a fraction of a second before pulling the little girl's undernourished body up against her.

Donnie turned. "Come on, Sabrina, this place is toxic. We need to get out of here and let the guys with the suits take over." She knew he meant the team that would come in to clean up the meth lab. Since they came from out of town, it would take them a while to get there. Sabrina reached for

Tony's hand, but he knelt and snagged the wallet on the floor. Donnie sighed with exasperation. "Come on, kid, it's dangerous in here. You can't take that with you. It's not yours."

Tony's jaw jutted. "Is too. Jordan said I'm 'posed to watch over it and make sure nothing happened to it."

Sabrina coughed. She needed fresh air. She nodded to Donnie, who took a step toward Tony just as the door opened and Clay stepped inside. The welt on his cheek looked as if it hurt. He looked at the foursome. "He got away, but officers are looking for him." Clay dropped in front of Tony. "Where are your mom and dad?"

Tony shrugged. "Don't got a dad. My mom's got a new boyfriend. I think she went with him somewhere." His lower lip trembled again. "Jordan's supposed to be taking care of us till she gets back."

Clay looked at Sabrina. "Where do they live?"

"On the edge of town about two miles from here."

"You want to try to get in touch with their mom?"

"Sure." She pulled her phone out. Tony and Maria had been in and out of the system once already.

There was no answer. She hung up and sighed. Then called her boss on her personal line.

Rachel Keys answered. "Hello?"

Sabrina filled her in on the situation and waited for Rachel's direction. For a moment Rachel was silent. Then she said, "I'll send someone out to the house. You get the kids to the hospital to get checked out, and I'll get back to you."

"Okay, just text me the address where they'll be staying. Thanks." She hung up and turned to the children. "Looks like you guys are going with me for a little while tonight. Is that all right?"

Maria smiled. Tony shrugged. It wasn't the first time he'd spent the night in a strange place. And at least he knew and trusted her. As much as he trusted anybody.

Clay shifted his attention to Tony. "Will you let me piggyback you out of here and get some ice cream?" Sabrina caught the subtle undercurrent of tension running through his words, but she didn't think Tony noticed. Without waiting for his consent, Clay dropped to his knees on the filthy floor. "Hop on."

"What about Jordan? What if he comes back? He told us to sneak out. We were going to run home. How will he find us now?"

Clay glanced at Sabrina. She touched the boy's head. "He knows how to find me, honey. He'll call me as soon as he can, I'm sure. I'll tell him where you are."

"Okay, if you're sure."

"I'm sure. I really am."

He stepped over to Clay. "Fine." He wrapped his bony arms around Clay's neck and crawled onto his back. Clay stood, and Sabrina felt relief sweep through her. The faster they got out, the better.

Within seconds, they were outside the trailer. Sabrina pulled in a breath of fresh air and wondered if she'd ever get the smell of the trailer out of her nose.

Other law enforcement continued their search for Stan Prescott. Sabrina hoped they found him soon. She stared at Clay as he talked to one of the other officers. Did he remember her? He was six years her senior and had graduated high school the year she turned twelve. He'd have no reason to remember *her*.

Although as soon as he'd heard her name, he'd probably remembered the rumors, the gossip, the snickers that had run rampant about her mother and his uncle. It hadn't mattered to Steven that her mother had left his uncle at the altar almost thirty years ago, but Sabrina knew some people had long memories. How long was Clay's?

Feeling Maria's warm body next to hers just brought home the unfairness of it all. And reminded her why she did what she did, took the chances she took. Sabrina's heart went out to these innocent children.

She walked to her car and opened the back door. Never knowing when she would have to transport a child, she had three different car seats—two in her trunk and one for Maria's age strapped into the seat. She untangled the child's arms from around her neck and settled her in the seat. She handed her a stuffed teddy bear. "Would you like a new friend?"

Maria hugged the bear while Tony slid into the seat next to her. Sabrina reached into the bag on the floor in front of Maria's feet and pulled out another bear and a fire truck. "Tony, would you like a new friend or a toy?"

Clay buckled the child in. Tony looked at the bear and the truck with equal longing. Sabrina moved the bear's face up close and tapped Tony's cheek with it as though offering a kiss. The boy smiled and ducked his head.

One grimy hand snagged the bear and tucked him under his chin. Sabrina set the truck next to him and turned to find Clay standing much too close. She couldn't back up and she didn't want to look silly scuttling sideways to put some distance between them.

She looked up, and her nose bumped his chin. She saw him swallow and was grateful when he stepped back a pace. "Are you taking them to the hospital?" he asked.

"Yes. I don't think there's anything seriously wrong with them that a few good meals and some vitamins won't fix, but I have to follow protocol."

Clay shook his head. "I'll follow you to the hospital." He ran a hand down his face in a weary gesture.

"You don't have to. We'll be fine."

Something flickered in his eyes as his gaze darted between the children, then back to her. "I want to talk to you about Steven."

Sabrina didn't know what he thought she could tell him but didn't have the energy to argue. "I'm taking them to Wrangler's General." It was a smaller hospital located in the center of town, but the staff was efficient. If something turned up and the kids needed more intensive care than she thought, then they would be transferred to a larger hospital in Nashville about an hour away. But she didn't think that was going to be necessary.

"I'll meet you there."

"Wait a minute, I need to show you something."

"What?" Clay frowned.

"Tony, would you show Clay the wallet Jordan asked you to hold on to for safekeeping?"

Tony narrowed his eyes, then shrugged and dug out the black wallet with the silver duct tape along the folded edge.

Clay gasped. "What?" He moved in for a closer look, then stumbled back without touching the wallet. He snagged his phone and punched in a number. "Yeah, Ned. I need you to get over to the Prescott trailer. Steven's wallet is here, and I can't bag it as evidence because of conflict of interest and all that, and I don't want anyone but you to do it."

Sabrina lifted a brow even as her heart hurt for him at the pain seeing the wallet brought him. When he hung up, he paced in front of the car while Sabrina explained to Tony that he would have to give the sheriff the wallet when he got here.

Tony didn't seem agreeable to that idea, but by the time the sheriff arrived ten minutes later, Tony had decided that Jordan would be okay with him giving it to the sheriff since no one could keep it more safe than he.

"Where is it?" Ned asked.

Sabrina nodded to Tony, who handed the wallet over to the sheriff. She gave the child's shoulder an approving squeeze.

She turned to Ned. "Steven's bought me enough cups of coffee over the past year that I knew it the moment I saw it. I even joked about getting him a new wallet for Christmas this year." Tears clogged her throat at the memories. "But he liked that one," she whispered.

"His wife gave it to him when they got married." The raw grief in Clay's voice sliced her heart. Steven had told her about his short marriage. He'd married his high school sweetheart the day after they'd graduated college. Two months later she'd been killed by a drunk driver while biking into town.

Clay cleared his throat and blinked fast. "Stan's got to know something about Steven's murder, which means finding him just moved into the number one spot on my priority list."

Ned squatted in front of Tony. "Son, do you know where your brother got this wallet?"

Tony's lips tightened. "He found it in the bedroom when he was on the phone with Ms. Sabrina. He grabbed it and said it didn't belong there and told me to hold it and make sure nothing happened to it." Anxiety filled his face. "You won't lose it, will you?"

Ned patted his head. "No, son, I promise I won't lose it."

"Jordan will be mad that I gave it to you." He bit his lip, and his brows dropped to the bridge of his nose.

Sabrina reached in and squeezed his hand. "No, hon, he'll be proud that you took care of it long enough to give it to someone who'll keep it safe."

Her words seemed to bring him a measure of comfort. He nodded and reached out a small finger to tap the badge on Ned's chest, then gave one more sharp nod. "Okay, then."

Clay shook his head. "My mother's cried buckets over that wallet. When it wasn't in his things the coroner had, she was inconsolable."

Sabrina touched his arm. "At least one good thing came out of this." She slid into the driver's seat and paused when her cell phone rang. "Hello?"

"Are you okay, Ms. Sabrina?"

"Jordan? Where are you? Why did you run and leave Maria and Tony behind? Why did you have them there in the first place?"

"They followed me. I didn't know they were there until— It doesn't matter. I— They said they wanted to play a practical joke on you. They said they'd pay me fifty bucks to call you out to the trailer and to be there waiting on you, but when I was on the phone with you I saw the wallet—"

Sabrina waved Clay over and mouthed, "It's Jordan." Back into the phone, she said, "Where are you? Who said they'd pay you?"

"I don't know, just a voice on the phone. But I saw Steven's wallet in the trailer and I...I figured Stan killed him. And they wanted you to come out there. They said it was a joke and they just wanted to talk to you, but after I saw the wallet, I didn't think it was just a joke. I was afraid they'd hurt you. That's why I told you not to come. I had to leave to make sure the guy followed me so Tony and Maria could get away. Are they okay? Please tell me they're all right."

"They're fine. Where are you?"

"I've got to disappear for a while. They're going

to be looking for me. I don't think my mom's coming back anytime soon, so take care of the kids."

She thought she heard a sob before the click. She swallowed hard as the reality of Jordan's words washed over her. Someone had set her up to come out to the trailer. Someone who had a dead officer's wallet in his bedroom. The chill that shook her had nothing to do with the temperature outside.

And everything to do with the fact that she thought she might be a target.

A target who might end up just like Steven Starke.

THREE

Twenty minutes later, they pulled into the parking lot of Wrangler's General.

Sabrina got out of the car and opened the back door to find Maria had fallen asleep. She eased the child out of the car seat. Maria stirred and settled her head on Sabrina's shoulder. Even though the little girl desperately needed a bath, Sabrina ignored that and snuggled her closer. Her heart tightened. Would she ever have a family of her own?

Now wasn't the time for those thoughts. She carried her into the hospital while Clay took charge of Tony, who'd gone silent and sullen.

Yet kept a tight grip on the stuffed animal.

Sabrina flashed her credentials to the triage staff. Lily Anderson, a nurse Sabrina had worked with who had become her best friend over the past year, stood when she saw her. "Sabrina, who do you have here?" She moved so she could get a look. "Ah. What a cutie."

"This is Maria Zellis. Her brother Tony is over

there. It looks like I'm going to take them to a foster home tonight. We can't locate their parents or the grandparents."

Lily turned in the direction Sabrina pointed and winced, grabbing her lower back.

"Are you all right?"

Lily nodded and blew out a slow breath. "Yes, it's just from that car accident I had about three years ago. Every once in a while, my back reminds me I'm not exactly the same."

"Is there anything you can do about it?"

"Not really. I do my physical therapy and just take it one day at a time." Lily's gaze moved behind Sabrina and she caught her breath again, this time in surprise.

"What is it?" Sabrina asked.

Lily nodded. "Well, well. Clay Starke. Dad said something about the town's bad boy coming home. Your mother isn't the only person to send the gossips around here into a feeding frenzy."

Sabrina flinched but didn't take offense. She focused on the duo. Clay and Tony were now headed straight for her. She looked at Lily. "Yes, I know Clay's reputation, but I'm not judging him because of it." She prayed he'd return the favor and wouldn't hold her mother's actions against her, either.

Lily grimaced. "I'm sorry. That was uncalled for. It's just he and my brother graduated together.

I remember Hank talking about Clay's escapades. They were the highlight of the week."

"You mean they took precedence over my mother's escapades?"

Lily flushed. "In my house they did." She sighed. "He may be a cop now, but most people in town will never let him live down the fact that he burned down Bryce England's house, leaving the boy scarred for life."

Clay saw the two women speaking in low voices, and he caught the occasional glance the pretty redhead threw at him.

Lily Anderson, Ned and Daisy Ann's daughter. She was friends with his sister and had been out to the ranch a few times to ride with Amber. She caught him watching and gave a smile. He couldn't tell if it was fake or the real thing. Tony's fascination with the hand-sanitizer dispenser had delayed their journey to the triage area. Now the child stayed snugged up to his side as Clay led him over to the two women. "Everything all right?"

Sabrina lifted a brow. "Of course."

Clay nodded to Lily. "Nice to see you again."

"Sorry to hear about your brother."

Pain shafted through him. He smiled anyway. "Appreciate that."

The door to the pediatric wing opened, and a

nurse with a clipboard stood there. She caught Sabrina's eye and gave a small nod. "Come on, let's get them back there," Sabrina said.

Tony's small fingers spasmed and Clay could feel the tension running through the child. He knelt in front of the little boy. "Are you scared?" he whispered.

Tony stuck out his jaw and he started to shake his head no, then changed midshake and nodded. "Yeah," he whispered back.

Clay rose and held out his arms. "Want me to carry you?"

"Uh-huh." Tony practically leaped into Clay's arms. He clutched the little boy and swallowed against the sudden lump growing in his throat.

He turned and found Sabrina watching him with a tender expression. Clay sucked in a deep breath and frowned. "Come on. Let's get this done. We've got things to talk about."

He knew his words sounded gruff, but Sabrina didn't look as if she took it to heart. She simply offered him a sad smile full of understanding. And something else. A new emotion in her eyes. But what? He didn't have time to figure it out. He cleared his throat and followed her through the double doors.

With the kids in good hands and Sabrina watching over them like a mother hen, Clay rubbed his weary eyes as he stepped away from the examination room. He pressed his phone to his ear and spoke to his boss. "I thought I'd be bored stiff being a cop in a small town. What'd y'all do to this place while I was gone?"

Ned gave a low chuckle. "When it's slow, it's slow, but the action does seem to come in waves."

"Well, right now we've got a tsunami." He sighed. "Have you found Prescott or Jordan Zellis yet?"

"No. We're still looking. I sent Lance out to Jordan's home, and it's dark as a tomb." Lance Goode was one of the other deputies in Wrangler's Corner. "We pinged his cell phone and found it in the bushes behind Prescott's trailer."

"So Jordan was pretty close by when he called."

"Yes. He probably saw Prescott coming his way and took off. May have dropped his phone while running."

"Or Prescott caught up with him," Clay said softly.

"Yes. Or that. I'm hoping he didn't."

"Maybe Lance will find something." Clay and Lance had gotten in minor trouble together as teens. He found it ironic they were now cops for the same town they used to want to escape from. "Keep me updated. I want to know why Jordan was in Prescott's trailer with Steven's wallet."

"Trust me, we all want to know that." Papers

shuffled. "I did get one piece of information. Jordan is good friends with a fellow named Trey Wilde."

"I don't know him."

"Stay around here long enough, and you will. His family moved here shortly after you left." He paused. "He reminds me of you in some ways at that age. Tough as nails, out to conquer the world, but with a wild streak a mile long. It's like he's trying to live up to his last name."

Clay couldn't help the small grimace at Ned's words. "Well, I'll keep that in mind when I run into him."

"Only thing about Trey is he's got money. And lots of it."

"So he's getting in trouble because...?"

"Who knows? I've talked with him a few times, but he doesn't seem to hear it. His daddy bails him out of trouble every time and Trey goes on his way to find more trouble." Ned sighed. "Anyway, I'll send someone to bring him in and see if he'll give us anything on Jordan. Be careful."

"Yeah." They hung up, and Clay turned to find Sabrina behind him looking at her phone. "Are you all right?"

"Yes. I'm just answering my boss." She finished the text and looked up with a shiver. "I've never had a day like today, but I think I'm okay. I'm definitely grateful no one's hurt, but I'm worried about Jordan."

Clay had the overwhelming urge to pull her into a hug and reassure her. He resisted and curled his fingers into fists. "All right, then. I've got a report to write. Do you need anything else?"

"No. Not tonight. Once we're finished here, I'll be taking the children to your parents' house."

Clay froze. "What?"

Sabrina lifted an eyebrow. "They're going to your parents'."

"Why would you take them there?"

She blinked. "Because they're the only foster family that has room for two kids right now."

Clay was stunned. He finally found his tongue. "I've been home four weeks, and my parents haven't said a word about being a foster home. When did they decide to do this?"

"They were cleared to foster just before Steven was killed. Maria and Tony Zellis will be their first kids."

Before he could respond, Dr. Gina Myers stepped from the room, leaving the door cracked so she could keep an eye on the children while she talked to Sabrina. "We're just waiting on some results from the tests, but I don't expect any surprises. I'm going to go ahead and release them so you can get them into a bed somewhere." She peeked through the crack. "Maria's sound asleep. I raised the rail on the bed so she won't fall if she rolls. Tony's lying next to her but is still awake." She handed Sabrina the discharge papers and shrugged. "Overall, other than needing three good meals a day, they're pretty healthy kids. I'm pleasantly surprised."

Sabrina nodded. "Good. I'll take care of them from here."

Clay rubbed his eyes. "Okay. I talked to Ned."

Hope flared in her expression. "Have they found Jordan?"

"No. Not yet. They will. And no sign of Stan Prescott either, but Ned's got someone watching his trailer and will nab him when he shows his face. But he did get the name of one of Jordan's friends."

"Who?"

"A guy by the name of Trey Wilde."

Sabrina frowned.

Clay raised a brow. "I take it you know him?"

"Yes. And while I never think a kid is beyond hope, I would say he's pretty borderline."

"What about Jordan?"

"There's hope for Jordan. He's got a good heart—as evidenced by the fact that he thought his siblings were in trouble and tried to lead that person away from them." She sighed. "He just needs direction, a man in his life who would take an interest and teach him."

Clay nodded. "Well, since you're heading my way, you want some help getting the kids in the car?"

"That would be great."

Fifteen minutes later, the kids were buckled in. Maria never opened her eyes. Tony leaned his head against the window, and Sabrina figured he'd be asleep by the time they arrived at the Starke ranch.

Sabrina pulled behind Clay and let him lead the way. As she drove, she prayed, thanking God for sparing all of them from Stan's craziness. Getting shot at, then having a gun held on her had been terrifying. Not just for herself but for the children. She thought it amazing that no one had been hurt and easily gave God the credit for that.

Sabrina pushed her Bluetooth device into her ear and dialed her grandmother's number.

"Hello?"

"Hi, Granny May."

"Sabrina, where are you, my girl?"

"I'm taking two children out to a foster home. It might be a while before I get home, but I didn't want you to worry."

Granny May had just turned seventy-two but had more energy than anyone Sabrina had ever met. She ran her bed-and-breakfast with a tender heart and a shrewd business mind. "I always worry about you when you're off on one of your assignments."

Sabrina didn't bother telling her grandmother she'd had every cause to worry on this one. "Don't worry. Just pray."

"All the time." A pause. "What am I praying for?"

"The children, Granny May." Sabrina thought about it. "And a prayer that Steven's murderer will be found." *And that I'm just overreacting in thinking that I could possibly be a target.*

"What are you mixed up in, Sabrina?" Granny May's sharp ears hadn't missed the new note in Sabrina's voice. She frowned.

"I'm mixed up in these kids' lives—you know that. I'll tell you about it soon, but extra prayers wouldn't hurt."

"'Course they wouldn't. I'll get right to it."

"See you in an hour or so." It got dark early these days. Not even five-thirty and already the sun rode low on the horizon. She hung up and followed Clay when he turned onto a gravel drive. They drove for about a half a mile before he pulled to a stop in front of a large two-story brick home with white columns and a front porch full of rocking chairs. Multicolored lights twinkled around the perimeter of the roof of the porch. They wrapped around the columns barbershop-style. Electric candles burned in the windows, and a large Christmas tree lit up the front window.

This was where Clay had grown up. How had

he ever left? She'd heard about the farm, of course, and knew where he lived but had never set foot on the property. She'd never had a reason to. And had had every reason to avoid it.

She stepped out of the car and the front door opened. A woman in her mid-fifties was followed by a man about the same age. Both looked excited and nervous at the same time. Maria and Tony would be their first experience with fostering. Sabrina sent up a quick prayer that it would be a good one.

"Clay, honey," Julianna said, "are y'all hungry?"

He must have called his mother on the way. "I am," Clay answered. "The kids are asleep, but if they wake up, they'll probably want something."

Sabrina stepped forward. "Thank you so much for being available to take in Maria and Tony," she said. She'd never had an extended conversation with Ross or Julianna Starke, but when in town, they exchanged polite nods.

Clay's father nodded, his eyes on the car. "You need some help carrying them in?"

"I got it, Dad, thanks." Clay opened the back door, unfastened Tony's seat belt and gently removed him from the car.

The boy stirred. "Where are we?"

"We're at your foster home, son."

"Don't want no foster home. Wanna go home with Jordan," he mumbled.

"Jordan can't take care of you right now, I'm afraid, but you'll like it here, I promise."

Tony woke further. "Where's Maria?"

"She's right here," Sabrina assured him. She had the little girl in her arms. Maria rubbed her face and laid her head on Sabrina's shoulder. To Clay's mother she said, "They both need baths and food and then I think they'll be ready for bed. They've had a very stressful day."

"Of course, of course. Bring them on in."

"They don't have any clothes." Sabrina stepped inside and the smell of fried chicken made her stomach growl. She ignored it. "If you can make do for tonight, I'll see what I can find at the community church first thing tomorrow." Wrangler's Corner Community Church had a food and clothing pantry. Sabrina had used it more than once to dress her charges.

"We'll be fine. When we decided to take in foster children, I asked for donations from friends and my church. We got a closetful in under two hours. I'm sure something will fit these little darlings. Now, come on into the kitchen and we'll get to know each other over dinner."

Sabrina hesitated. "I don't want to intrude." But she didn't want to just drop the kids and leave, either. Maria had already gotten attached to her. She wondered if Clay's parents realized who she was. They had to, and yet they were treating her with a kindness she hadn't expected. She'd been friends with Steven, of course, but had gone out of her way to avoid the rest of his family. Shame gripped her.

"Wouldn't be intruding," Clay said. "I'm going to run up and wash my hands. You want to come with me, Tony?"

The little boy looked at his grubby hands. "I probably need to."

A smile played on Clay's lips. "Then come on."

Tony paused and looked at his sister. "You, too, Maria. You're just as dirty as I am."

Maria stirred. She looked at Clay's mother. "You got ice cream?"

Mrs. Starke smiled. "I sure do. What kind do you like?"

"Neo-poppin'."

Confusion filled the woman's face. Sabrina translated, "I think she means Neapolitan."

"Ah, well, that clears it up. And it just happens we do have it."

Maria grinned.

The front door banged shut, and Sabrina jumped, her arms tightening around the little girl, who wiggled to get down. She set her on the floor, and Maria walked over to take her brother's hand. Sabrina forced herself to relax. Her nerves were shot, and she needed to decompress.

Heavy boots clomped toward the kitchen. A man who could have been Ross Starke's twin appeared in the doorway. He held a rifle in his left hand and a bag of apples in his right. He set the apples on the floor and leaned the rifle against the wall. "Saw a couple of deer over this way and thought I'd bag me one. Went back and got my rifle and now I can't find the deer." He looked around. "Hey, Clay, saw you drive up. What's going on?"

Sabrina tensed, her stomach twisting into a knot. Abe Starke. A man she'd spent her life avoiding now stood three feet from her.

"Uncle Abe. My parents have decided to take in foster kids. This is Tony and that's Maria."

Abe gave a smart bow and held out his hand. "Pleasure to meet you two."

Maria giggled and ducked her head. Tony's lips curved slightly as he shook Abe's large hand.

Abe looked back up. "Julianna, I brought those tables over for the barbecue."

"Oh, great. Clay can help you take them into the barn until we need to set them up."

Abe's gaze finally landed on Sabrina, and he froze. The warmth in his eyes frosted over. "What's she doing here?"

Julianna gasped. "Abe Starke, that was rude."

He snorted. "Yeah? Well, I thought it was pretty rude when her mother left me standing at the altar." His eyes lasered into Sabrina, who stood frozen. "You're not welcome in this house—or on this land, for that matter. Get out."

FOUR

Clay recoiled as though his uncle had slugged him. He'd heard the sad story his entire life, but he hadn't realized Abe still harbored such strong bitterness. He'd been gone too long.

His mother sucked in a deep breath. "Not here, Abe."

"Then where, Julie?" Abe glared at his sister-in-law.

Tony's and Maria's gazes swung from one adult to the next. Sabrina stepped forward and placed a hand on Maria's head. "I think I'll go." She sounded shaky. Unsure. Confused. But Clay knew she wouldn't say anything or ask questions in front of the children.

He shot a look at his mother, who quickly gathered the two children and two plates of food and ushered them out of the kitchen and down the hall. Thankfully, they went without protest.

Clay stared at his uncle. "This isn't the time or the place. Let the past stay in the past."

Abe pointed at Sabrina. "You knew who she was and you brought her here?"

Clay tried to put a lid on his impatience. "Yes, of course. She didn't have anything to do with what her mother did. It's time to let it go, Abe."

Clay thought he detected a bit of steam leaking from his uncle's ears, but he was sick and tired of the whole "feud," the animosity and antagonism displayed toward Sabrina and her grandmother—two innocent women.

Clay's attention circled back to Sabrina.

She stood frozen, lips tight, face pale. She stiffened her spine and squared her shoulders. "I haven't seen my mother in about twenty years. I don't know where she is or if she's even still alive." She glanced toward the door where the children had disappeared, then looked at his uncle Abe. "I'm sorry for what she put you through."

"Sorry? Sorry about the fact that your mama and I were engaged to be married and she never showed up?" He snorted and gave a humorless laugh. "Or sorry about the fact that she did show up about two years late?" He slammed a fist into the wall. Clay winced and Sabrina jumped. "It wasn't enough she left me at the altar, but then she humiliates me by coming back to town with a baby in tow. A baby that's obviously not mine."

"Me," she whispered.

"Yeah. You. So you can see why you're not welcome in this house."

"But I'm not my mother." She straightened her back and met Abe glare for glare.

"Close enough."

Sabrina flinched. "I've worked very hard to prove myself in this town. I'm not her. I'll never be her."

Clay stepped in. "That's enough, Abe. Sabrina's never done anything to you. Knock it off."

"You stay out of it if you know what's good for you, boy." Abe curled his lip. "Looks like you're making all kinds of bad decisions these days. You can't come home to help your brother out, but you can take up with the likes of her? Not while I've got breath in my body. You won't do this to the family." He shot Sabrina one last bitter look, walked to the kitchen door that led to the outside and slammed it behind him.

Silence reigned in the bright kitchen. Clay looked at his father and his father looked at him.

"What did Abe mean by that?" his dad asked.

"By what?"

"About you not being willing to come home and help Steven with whatever he was working on."

Clay sighed. "I'll have to explain that later." He turned to Sabrina, who stared at the wall. The stunned expression on her face broke his heart. "I didn't realize he would be here or I wouldn't have brought you. I'm sorry."

"You don't have anything to apologize for. I messed up. I should have done things different. I should have called." She looked surprised at her own admission.

He shook his head. "Come on. I'll see you get home."

She blinked and pulled in a deep breath. "I want to say good night to the children, if that's all right. I don't want to be another adult in their lives who just disappears."

Clay nodded. "Of course." He was amazed. His uncle had just been about as rude as a person could be, and she still had the children at the forefront of her mind.

He led her to the back of the house, where he found his mother sitting on the side of the bed with the children tucked into the queen bed in the guest room. She looked up when they peered in. Worry lines creased her forehead and her mouth. Her eyes met his in question. He forced a smile. "How's everything in here?"

"They each have a room if they want it, but they wanted to stay together tonight."

Sabrina nodded. "That's understandable for now." She hugged the children, promising to visit soon.

Clay gathered the empty dishes. "I'll put these in the kitchen on the way out."

His mother's hand captured Sabrina's. "You're welcome here anytime, my dear."

Sabrina bit her lip and nodded. "Thank you."

They walked from the room, and Sabrina seemed to be moving on autopilot. He saw his uncle's rifle still leaning against the wall. He snagged it. Outside, he saw her shiver and tug her heavy coat tighter. She nodded at the weapon. "What are you going to do with that?"

"Give it back to him when I have a serious talk with him." He touched her arm. "Are you all right?"

"Not really. I knew the story, of course. That she'd left Abe Starke at the altar. But even in a small town, it's possible to avoid someone. I've never spoken to your uncle until tonight. I've seen him in town, but not often."

"He's pretty much a hermit. His ranch borders my parents'. He and my dad help each other out whenever they need it. Uncle Abe hates going into town and only does so for the occasional doctor's appointment or to get supplies."

"I'm so sorry she hurt him like that." She sniffed and swiped a tear. "The kids certainly teased me enough about it when I was younger that I built him up to be a monster. Today I realized he's not a monster, just a very bitter, angry man."

"He's been that way all my life." He paused, then asked, "Why would the kids tease you about it? How would they even know who your mother was?"

She eyed him as if he'd lost his mind. "You've been gone a long time from here, haven't you?"

Clay shifted, uneasy. "Yeah, a little over ten years."

"Surely ten years couldn't wipe out your knowledge of how small towns operate."

He felt a flush creep into his neck. "I guess the people your mother went to school with kept the stories alive."

"You got it in one. Nothing else to talk about around here, I guess. They warned their kids about me, told them not to associate with the daughter of a—well, I'll let you fill in the blank. Needless to say, it wasn't a good time for me."

He nodded and scuffed a toe against the ground. "I remember hearing stuff, of course, but you were six years behind me. I really didn't pay that much attention." And he'd been dealing with his own problems. "Who's your father, Sabrina?"

She barked a harsh, short laugh. "Don't worry—it's not your uncle."

He grimaced. That hadn't been what he meant. At least he didn't think so. "Then who?"

She sighed, ran her hand down her face, then looked up at the sky. "Someone she met after she was engaged. Apparently, she chickened out of telling your uncle she didn't want to marry him and chose to leave town the morning of the wedding. She later told my grandmother that she was afraid of Abe, of his hair-trigger temper. She was too scared to tell your uncle she didn't want to get married, so she just ran. I guess she met my father shortly after that and got pregnant with me. My grandmother won't talk about my father much, just that he died in a car wreck when I was about a year old. My mother tried to make it on her own, but she couldn't, so she came back to Wrangler's Corner. With me in tow."

"Where she became the talk of the town."

"Well, she didn't exactly have a sterling reputation before she pulled the leaving-your-uncle-at-the-altar stunt. But she didn't help things when she came back. She got into drugs, attached herself to any man who would spend money on her and landed in jail more times than I can remember." She swallowed hard. "And she ruined any chance of a happy childhood for me."

Sabrina clenched her jaw against the flood of memories. The bullying, the cruel teasing by the other children. She knew they were simply mimicking their parents, but it still hurt. Her grandmother had done her best to shelter her, but she'd never lived down her mother's reputation Not everyone had been so awful, of course, but there had been enough of them to leave permanent scars.

And now she knew why her grandmother had been as antsy as a cat in a roomful of rocking chairs whenever Sabrina mentioned spending time with Steven Starke. She was afraid people would talk and all the gossip would rev up again. Sabrina found herself cringing at the thought. "I want to go home." She climbed in her car and started the engine.

Clay tapped on her window and with a sigh, she pressed the button to lower it.

He leaned toward her. "I'm going to follow you, make sure you get there safely."

"That's not necessary. It's a fifteen-minute ride into town, and then you'll just have to come back."

"I'm following you."

She studied the determination in his eyes, the stubborn set to his jaw. She warmed under his gaze. He cared. Or at least she thought he did. "Fine."

He hefted the rifle. "Just let me walk over to my house and lock this up. Then we can go." He started to walk away, then turned back. "One more question."

She lifted an eyebrow.

"Will you get something to eat with me?"

Sabrina blew out a small breath that was a cross between a sigh and a tired laugh. His uncle's ugly words were still there, but they didn't sting as much right now. "Sure." Why not? She was hungry.

He looked around. "I'd say let's just eat here, but I don't know where my uncle went or if he's coming back, and I'd just as soon not be here if he does."

"I get it." Sabrina backed out and waited for Clay to put the rifle away, climb into his cruiser and pull in behind her. She led the way from the ranch, out of the valley and onto the road that would take them into town. As she drove, her mind spun.

Abe Starke had been the man her mother had left at the altar. Of course she knew that. It was one reason she avoided the man if at all possible, making sure their paths never crossed. If she saw him in town, she went the other way. Tonight had been the first time she and Abe had ever exchanged words. She sighed.

For the most part, all Sabrina had ever cared about was staying out of the way of the bullies and the gossips, doing her best to close her ears—and her heart—to what people said. And her grandmother never talked about it.

She pushed the topic from her mind to think about another subject that was almost just as painful. Steven Starke.

She pulled into the parking lot of the bed-and-breakfast, the home she shared with her grandmother. Clay drove three doors down across the street to park in front of the diner. She smiled at his good fortune. Parking was often hard to find on Main Street, so she didn't bother to try. She had to come back to the bed-and-breakfast after she was finished eating anyway. Sabrina crossed the street and hit the sidewalk that led down to the front of the diner.

Clay got out of his car as she approached. "I want to talk to you about Steven," he said. "I didn't realize you two knew each other."

She'd figured that might be something he'd bring up. So the topic of her mother and his uncle was shelved for now. She was glad about that. Not so glad that he was asking about Steven. "He was a good cop and a good friend. He talked about you a lot." She smiled. "He was proud of you and your big detective job in Nashville."

He flushed, and his eyes turned red. He blinked. "Were you at his funeral?"

"Yes," she whispered.

"I didn't see you."

"And I didn't see you." The church had been packed. She felt her own tears try to surface and fought them as she did every time she thought about Steven. "I was at the back, near the door." She walked to the glass door of the diner, trying to get her emotions under control. Clay came up behind her to open the door for her. She stepped into the warmth and pulled her hands from her coat pocket.

"Sabrina, honey, how are you?"

Sabrina had to smile. "I'm fine, Daisy Ann." Daisy Ann Anderson was one of Sabrina's favorite people. Married to Sheriff Ned Anderson and mother to Lily, Daisy Ann had been running the diner since before Sabrina had been born. In her mid-fifties, she was slim and trim and carried herself with the poise of a model. She was also one who didn't judge Sabrina based on her mother's past. "I just saw Lily at the hospital."

Daisy Ann's lips tightened. "She's had some horrific hours lately. Girl is working too much."

"And with her back bothering her so much. Poor thing. I'll be praying for her."

"You do that, honey. Lord knows she needs the prayers." Sorrow glinted. Then her eyes widened when they landed on Clay. "Well, I heard you'd come back to town. I wondered when you'd find your way in here."

Clay gave the woman a hug. "Hi, Mrs. J." He looked around. "Kinda slow tonight?"

Daisy Ann's face shuttered. "It's slow most nights these days." Sabrina winced. She knew the diner had taken a hit with the recent loss of jobs when the textile plant two towns over closed. People weren't eating out so much in Wrangler's Corner. "Y'all just take a seat. I'll bring coffee."

Sabrina led Clay to a corner booth where she could see the door. The diner wasn't completely empty, but it was far from booming. "I don't know how she stays open, Clay."

"It's a shame. This place is a landmark."

"I know. I eat here every chance I get."

Daisy Ann had only one other waitress working and soon Sabrina and Clay clasped two mugs of decaf coffee, his with cream and sugar and hers black. "I heard your parents are still doing the barbecue," Daisy Ann said.

"Yes, there wasn't any question in their minds. They do it every year and figured Steven would insist on it," Clay said.

Grief flickered in her eyes and she blinked back tears. "He did like his barbecue."

"This year will be a hard one. I expect Mom to cry through the whole thing, but she'll do it." He studied her. "All the guys at the station are talking about turning it into a memorial to Steven. There's even talk about some of the wives putting together an auction to raise money for families of officers killed in the line of duty."

"That would be wonderful. Steven would be proud." Daisy Ann patted his shoulder and headed back toward the kitchen.

Clay looked at Sabrina. "What are you thinking?"

"That I messed up and I don't know what to do about it. I don't make mistakes like that."

"Like what?"

"Like not calling ahead and telling your parents who I was. Like not waiting on the police to arrive before I decided to go in the trailer. Like—"

"You weren't thinking of yourself when you did those things. That's not messing up—that's putting others first."

She opened her mouth, then closed it. Opened it again. And shut it again.

"What? I've rendered you speechless?"

"Yes. A bit." She relaxed a fraction. "But you've definitely given me something to think about. I've worked so hard to have a good reputation in this town. I don't want to do anything to blow it."

"Your reputation matters so much?"

She frowned. "Of course."

"As long as you're doing the right thing, what does it matter what other people think?"

She cleared her throat. "I know that's the way it should work, but with my mother's past and the way people still look at me sometimes—as though just waiting for me to prove I'm like her..." She lifted a shoulder in a slight shrug. "It just matters, okay?"

"Fair enough." Clay fingered the saltshaker, then set it down with a thump. "Do you have any idea at all who killed Steven?"

She leaned back, and her frown deepened. She felt the tension returning to her shoulders. "No. Don't you think if I knew something I would have told someone by now?"

"Of course. Of course." He raked a hand through his hair. "I'm sorry. It was a dumb question."

"Yes. It was." Sabrina paused. She stared at her coffee. "Steven was my friend, too."

"I know. I'm sorry."

She waved a hand. "I'm tired and feeling a little defensive tonight. I don't know who killed him. I truly don't have any idea. His death stunned me. I will say I think your first place to start is with Stan Prescott and Steven's wallet, but…"

"But what?"

"There may be something else." She sighed. "I spoke to Steven the day before he died."

Clay tensed and leaned forward, his gaze boring into her as though he could see inside her head to grab her thoughts. "What did he say?"

"It wasn't really what he said—it was more what *I* told *him*."

"Which was?"

She stared at him. Did she dare tell him one of her deepest fears?

Clay leaned in. "Just say it, Sabrina."

"I think—" She paused. "I think I may have sent your brother to his death."

FIVE

She blurted the words, then bit her lip and reared back against the booth as though she thought he might hit her.

Clay didn't move for a split second. Then he sucked in a steadying breath. "What?"

She dipped her head, then reached up to pinch the bridge of her nose. "That was a really bad way to put it."

"Tell me."

"As they say, hindsight is twenty-twenty. The day before he died, we talked. I told him about a family I'm working with. Jordan's family."

He stiffened. "Tony and Maria's family."

"Yes.

"The mom has custody, but they stay with their grandparents sometimes. I couldn't get ahold of them tonight, which is why the kids are with your parents."

"Okay."

"The mom just got custody back and I make regular visits to check in on them, but that day I was going to see if Maria wanted to come be a part of the church play. They don't live too far and—" She waved a hand. "Anyway, when I got there, Jordan wasn't home, but Maria took me back to her bedroom. When I passed Jordan's room, I thought I saw some kind of pipe on his dresser."

"Okay."

"Knowing the history of drug abuse in the family, I asked Steven to investigate it. Quietly. Because if it wasn't true, I didn't want to isolate the family. They were just starting to trust me, and if I were to start accusing their grandson of using or dealing drugs, all of my hard work would be down the drain."

Daisy Ann placed a platter of fries in front of them along with two hamburgers and a chocolate shake neither had ordered. "What's this, Daisy Ann?" Sabrina asked.

"You know Billy. He said you needed fattening up." She turned to Clay. "I just happen to like you." She shrugged. "Milk shakes are on the house." She put two straws on the table and Sabrina tried to will the flush to stay out of her cheeks.

Daisy Ann left and Sabrina concentrated on her hamburger.

"Fattening up?" Clay asked.

Sabrina snorted. "And she likes you. How about that?" She sighed and put her hamburger down.

She wiped her mouth. "Billy's like a father to me. He thinks I don't eat enough and every time I come in here, he sends something fattening over to me. Looks like Daisy Ann thinks you deserve equal treatment."

Clay's gaze roamed her features. "Well, I think you're just about perfect, if my judgment's worth anything," he said softly.

The flush swept into her cheeks and there wasn't one thing she could do about it. She cleared her throat. "Thanks."

His softness disappeared. He shook his head. "So what did Steven say?"

"That he would check on it."

"And?"

"And he came by my house that night. He said he thought I might be right, that something was going on in this town that was bigger than either of us imagined. I asked him what. He said he didn't want to say anything yet, but he'd tell me soon. Then the next day he was dead," she whispered. She met his gaze. Tears swam to the surface and she blinked. "Was it my fault? Is he dead because I asked him to look into it?"

Clay drew in a deep breath. "Of course it's not your fault. He's dead because some lowlife killed him." He wiped his mouth. "But if there's a connection between your request and the reason he's dead, you can be sure I'm going to find out."

"I later asked Jordan about the pipe, and at first he said it was his. I told him I knew it wasn't, because I'd seen him a lot and he hadn't been high. He finally confessed that it belonged to his mother, but he said he told her to get rid of it and she did." She paused. "I'm still not sure that's the truth, but I'm willing to give him the benefit of the doubt for now."

Sabrina could tell his mind was on the family she'd just told him about. He asked for the address and she gave it to him. "You're not officially investigating Steven's death, are you?"

"Nope. I've been forbidden. Conflict of interest and all that."

"But you're going to talk to them anyway, aren't you?"

He hesitated. "We'll see. I want to at least be there even if I'm not the one officially asking questions." He tapped his lip. "Will the kids go back to the grandparents' house?"

She shook her head. "Not if I can help it. Last time they said it was too much for them." She bit her lip, then blew out a soft sigh. "Let me go with you when you talk to them. They're more likely to talk to you if I'm there."

He studied her for a second. "All right."

"Good." She nodded, then couldn't hold back the gigantic yawn. She covered her mouth. "I'm sorry. It's not the company, I promise."

He gave her a slow smile. "I understand."

They finished their food, and Sabrina sat back. Exhausted didn't begin to describe how she felt. But she couldn't ignore a niggling question that had bothered her ever since they'd left the hospital. "Lily brought up something I've wondered about for a long time. Steven wouldn't talk about it, but…"

"But what?"

"What happened with Bryce England? I have a hard time believing you would burn down his house." Clay froze and all the color bleached from his face. "Judging by your reaction, I'd say you probably don't want to talk about that, so just forget I asked."

It took him a moment, but he found his voice. "You're right. I don't talk about that." He placed a few bills on the table. "Dinner's on me." He stood. "I'll be in touch."

Then he was out the door before she could blink.

Okay, so that was definitely the wrong topic to bring up. Sabrina sat alone a few more minutes sipping on the milk shake and wishing she'd kept her mouth shut. When she'd slurped the last drop, she looked up to see Billy grinning at her from behind the counter. She rolled her eyes. "If I wind up with a weight problem, I'm sending you the diet-plan bill."

Billy chuckled. "You do that, Brina. I'm sure

I look like I'm worried." His dark features con-
trasted with his white T-shirt. He kept a bandanna
wrapped around his Afro. His chocolate-colored
eyes snapped with good humor and caring.

"No more milk shakes, Billy."

"Right, darling. I gotcha."

Sabrina knew the next time she came in, he'd
have one waiting for her. She sighed and rose,
looked around the diner and dropped a ten on the
table. She knew the diner was struggling and as
much as she appreciated the sweet treat, she would
make sure she did her part to keep the place open.
She caught Daisy Ann's eye. "See you tomorrow,
Daisy Ann."

Daisy Ann nodded, then frowned. "That yours?"

Sabrina looked at the floor. Clay's phone had
slipped out of his pocket. She snatched it up and
raced to the door.

She pushed through the glass door and stood on
the sidewalk. He was nowhere in sight, of course.
Sabrina stuck the phone in her pocket. He'd miss
it soon enough and come looking for it.

A cold wind sent shivers up her spine, but she
breathed deep.

Growing up in Wrangler's Corner had been hard.
She'd hated the small town for most of her life and
had been desperate to get away. But her grandmother needed her. At least that was what she told
herself. The one time she decided to take off on

her own had turned into disaster. And just like her mother, Sabrina had come home, tail tucked, defeat a weight she couldn't seem to shake. She shuddered. She didn't want to be anything like her mother.

A footstep behind her caught her attention, and she turned. She frowned at her jumpiness. There wasn't anyone behind her who looked suspicious. Her gaze roamed from face to face. A young couple strolling hand in hand, three teens window-shopping and enjoying the chilly night, and an older couple on the bench under the lamppost.

Nothing that should set her nerves on edge. And yet they were. Sabrina drew in a breath as the hair on her arms raised into goose bumps even beneath her heavy down coat.

The bed-and-breakfast, well lit and welcoming, lay ahead of her up and across the street.

She kept walking down the sidewalk, noting the businesses closed for the day. Few people were on the street and in the cold. She glanced behind her again and saw a young man and woman come out of an antiques store. The interior lights went off. The couple climbed into a red truck and pulled away from the curb.

Sabrina hunched her shoulders against the wind and quickened her pace.

Footsteps picked up behind her once again.

She spun in time to see a figure duck into a side alley near the doughnut shop.

Her stomach twisted.

She wasn't being jumpy.

Someone was following her.

Clay stepped on the brakes. His phone was missing. He'd reached for it to call his parents and found his pocket empty. Glad he'd discovered that fact only about half a mile from the restaurant, he checked his mirrors, then did a quick three-point turn.

He tapped the wheel, his mind spinning with several different topics. Bryce England. He didn't want to think about him. The fire had been ruled an accident, but that didn't help assuage the guilt that weighed heavy on Clay's shoulders every time he thought about it. So he wouldn't think about it. He had other things that had to take priority.

He had a lead on Steven's murder, and he had to decide what to do with it. He knew he should turn it over to Ned, but Clay wanted to talk to the family himself. If he told Ned what Sabrina had revealed, Ned would refuse to let him get anywhere near that family.

His conscience warred with his desire to be at the center of the investigation. He turned onto Main Street and thought he saw Sabrina hurry across the street toward her home. What was she still doing out? He would have thought she'd have been tucked inside the B and B long before now.

A figure darted behind her and, when she spun, ducked next to the building.

Clay frowned. Was he following her?

Sabrina made it to the porch of the B and B and turned once again to look over her shoulder.

Nothing moved. If someone was following her, he stayed hidden. Clay flipped on his blue lights. Sabrina jerked to look toward him. Fear mingled with relief showed on her face even though he knew she couldn't see him.

Clay caught movement from his passenger window and saw a dark-clad figure slip away into the night. He climbed from his vehicle and gave chase.

"Hey! Police! Stop!"

Clay could hear the person's fleeing footsteps for a brief moment, then silence. He pulled his weapon and went in search.

The man had darted down Johnson Street. A one-way road about the width of an alley. Clay called it in, requesting one of the deputies to meet him. Lance Goode, the one officer on the force who had seemed glad to have him take Steven's place, responded. "En route."

"He cut through on Johnson and may come out on Henry. Keep an eye out. He's small and wiry and obviously knows this area."

"Ten-four."

Clay turned his radio way down and moved forward on silent feet. The suspect knew he was being chased, but Clay wanted to be able to hear without the white noise obliterating anything that would signal danger.

Ears tuned, senses sharp, Clay headed down the street, weapon drawn. "Show yourself!"

A scrape behind him. He whirled.

Saw the pebbles glinting in the dim streetlight. And knew he'd fallen for one of the oldest tricks in the book. Distract and strike.

He ducked and swiveled around. Too late.

The metal trash-can lid caught him in the side of the head.

Pain shot through him, and he went to his knees. His weapon clattered on the ground, and he ignored the pain long enough to roll for it. Running footsteps faded down the street. Darkness threatened. He thought he heard Sabrina call his name.

Then Lance was there. "Clay!"

Clay shook off the ringing in his ears and swallowed at the pounding that now throbbed through his head, making him nauseous. "Ugh." He managed to holster the gun before collapsing back against the ground.

"Clay," Sabrina whispered, and dropped beside him. "Are you all right?"

"Yeah. Yeah." His vision finally steadied, and he held a hand up to Lance, who pulled him to his feet. Dizziness and nausea hit him all over again, and he swayed.

"I'll call 911," Sabrina said.

"No," Clay croaked. "No, I'll be all right." He looked at Lance. "I guess he got away."

"Yeah. Disappeared into the night. I never saw him. Heard the clang and your holler and came running."

"Great." Clay drew in a deep breath. His head still swam.

"Come on into the house and lie down for a minute," Sabrina said.

He wanted to protest, to climb in his car and go searching for the person who'd clocked him, but his head and stomach rebelled at the thought.

He let the two of them lead him to the B and B, up the front steps and into the foyer.

"Sabrina, what's going on?"

The high-pitched voice had to belong to Sabrina's grandmother. Clay heard Sabrina respond but couldn't seem to register the words. He just wanted to be horizontal as soon as possible.

Lance must have sensed the urgency and helped him to the nearest couch. Clay eased himself down and couldn't stop the low groan that escaped when he reclined.

Sabrina hurried to his side, an ice bag clutched in her hand. "Here." When she placed it on his head, he winced but left it there. "You really need to see a doctor."

"Did you know someone was following you?"

"I thought so." Her frown deepened. "But right now I want to make sure you're going to be all right. You're in no condition to drive."

"I can take him home," Lance said.

Clay snorted. "I'm not leaving my car."

"My granddaughter is right. You need a doctor. I'll call Daniel. He'll come right over." She hurried off, and Clay groaned again. Not in pain but because he knew he'd be seeing the doctor. He glanced at Sabrina. "A house call? Who does that these days?"

"Everyone owes Granny May a favor." She shrugged. "Besides, she's right. You need someone to look at your head."

Clay bit back another protest. He knew it wouldn't matter. Besides, he had another worry to deal with. "Lance, would you be willing to work with me on something?"

Lance eyed him. "Depends on what you're talking about."

The other six deputies in the department hadn't been exactly welcoming when they'd learned the sheriff had asked him to fill Steven's position on a temporary basis. Steven had been one of them, and his loss grieved them in a big way. Just because

Clay was his brother, didn't mean they wanted him there.

Familiar guilt hit Clay, and he took a deep breath. He had to do the right thing. "I'm talking about a lead on Steven's murder."

Lance's eyes narrowed. "What kind of a lead?"

Clay ignored the throbbing across the right side of his head and focused on Lance. He sensed he had Sabrina's full attention, too. "I mean, Steven went to see a family the day before he died. He was checking to see if the grandson was into drugs. Turns out the pipe belonged to the kid's mother. At least that's his story."

"Which family?"

"The Zellis family." Recognition flashed across Lance's face. Clay shifted the ice pack. "You know them?"

"Yeah. I busted their mom for meth. The kids went into the system before being placed with the grandparents." He looked at Sabrina. "Didn't the mom just get them back?"

"Yes. Only now she's taken off with her current boyfriend, leaving her drug paraphernalia—and children—behind."

Clay wondered if Lance would be the best one for the job. "I want you to check out this new lead."

Lance studied him. "All right."

Clay cocked a brow. "All right?"

"I'll check it out, but what's the catch?"

His friend had always been sharp. "I want to go with you."

Lance shook his head. "You can't work on this case."

"I'll sit in the car."

"No."

"I have to." Clay slammed a fist on his thigh and flinched as the action made his head vibrate.

"No. You don't." Lance spread his hands. "I mean, what's the point?"

If it didn't hurt so bad, Clay would have clenched his jaw. Instead he blew out a sigh. "The point is, I'll be close by. I need to do this for Steven."

Lance rubbed his chin. "For Steven or for yourself?"

Anger rose up in Clay, but he clamped it down. He supposed it was a legitimate question. "Maybe for both of us. I wasn't there for him when he was alive. Don't try to stop me from doing what I've got to do now that he's dead."

"My offer still stands," Sabrina said. "I'll go with you. The grandparents like me. The mom doesn't, but sounds like she's not around anyway."

Lance sighed and looked at Clay. Clay stared back, his face implacable. Lance threw his hands up. "All right, all right. I'll do it." He narrowed his eyes at Clay. "But you have to promise to stay in the car."

"I promise. I just… I need to be there."

Lance's phone buzzed, and he pulled it from his pocket. When he glanced at the number, he rolled his eyes.

"Who is it?" Clay asked. He shifted with a grunt and grabbed his head.

"Be still before you do more damage," Granny May ordered.

"Yes, ma'am."

Lance slipped his phone back into his pocket. "It's Krissy. She's been calling me all night," he muttered. "Bugging me to death about going to some concert in Nashville next weekend and I'm supposed to be working."

"Krissy?" Sabrina asked.

"My wife. I'll call her back in a few minutes."

"Go with her," Clay said. "I'll take your shift."

Lance blinked. "You will?"

"Sure. I figure I owe you." He shrugged, then winced. "But I'd do it anyway to help a man keep his wife happy."

Lance grunted. "It's taking a lot to keep her happy these days."

The doorbell cut the sudden awkward silence, and Granny May hustled to answer it. Sabrina guessed it was Daniel Billings, one of the doctors who looked up to her grandmother and had adopted her as his own. She heard his deep voice come from the foyer and then Granny May led him into the room. Tall enough to be a pro basketball player, he was in his early thirties with black hair and blue eyes.

He spotted Clay on the couch. "What'd you run into?"

"It's more like what ran into me."

"A metal trash-can lid got him," Sabrina offered.

Daniel raised his eyebrows. "People still use those?"

"Apparently."

He nodded to Sabrina. "Good to see you."

Sabrina offered him a friendly smile. "You, too, Daniel. Thanks for coming." His gaze lingered, and she cleared her throat. "Does he have a concussion?"

Daniel moved to the couch. "Why don't y'all give the guy a little privacy instead of hovering like a bunch of mother hens?"

Clay gave what Sabrina thought was supposed to be a smile but looked more like a grimace. Granny May ushered everyone out.

Sabrina stood in the kitchen with Lance. "What time do you want to go see the Zellises?"

"Why don't you call first thing in the morning and see what time they'll be home?"

She nodded. "If we go around nine o'clock in the morning, we should be fine. That's usually when they're home. I don't know why I couldn't reach them tonight."

"Sounds good."

"Has your life been too boring lately, my dear?" Granny May asked.

Sabrina looked back to find her grandmother coming into the kitchen. She flushed. "No, ma'am, I can't say it's been boring."

"What's going on, darling?"

Sabrina sighed. "I'll fill you in when everything calms down."

Daniel walked up behind her grandmother. She turned. "How's the patient?"

"Stubborn," he grunted. "But he'll be all right if he takes it easy. He must have a pretty hard head, because I don't see any signs of a concussion right now. He needs to be watched during the night. If he starts showing any signs of a concussion, I'd want to see him right away."

"I'll be all right. I've got to get home. Thanks for coming out like this. I appreciate it." Clay stood in the doorway, eyes squinted against the light.

Daniel shook his head. He looked at Granny May. "I've told him he's not to drive, so if he wants to go home, someone needs to take him. Or pick him up."

"I'll call Julianna and Ross," her grandmother said. Sabrina's brows rose. Granny May was on a first-name basis with Clay's parents?

"No," Clay said. "I don't want to worry my parents. They have enough going on right now. I'll be fine."

Enough going on? With the kids or dealing with his bitter uncle? She frowned. Snarkiness wasn't usually her nature.

"Then stay here," Granny May said. "No reason you can't use one of the empty guest rooms. I've got a T-shirt and shorts left from my husband you can use to sleep in."

"If you try to drive, I'll call your father," Daniel said, his tone mild, eyes serious.

Clay scowled, then dropped his head with a resigned sigh. Then he winced and lifted a hand to the bruise on his cheek. "All right." He looked at Granny May. "I guess you've got another guest for the night."

Granny May smiled. "Then come on. I'll show you your room and get you settled. It's just the Flemmings on the third floor and me and Sabrina. We've got plenty of room tonight."

Clay caught Sabrina's eye and she lifted her hands in a "What can you do?" gesture. He gave a light snort and followed her grandmother down the hall to one of the back bedrooms. Private and quiet with a king bed and an intercom system. She heard Granny May say, "And I'll check on you at least once to make sure you wake up."

"Yes, ma'am."

Sabrina showed the others out, closed the door

and leaned against it. *Lord, I've got a feeling something's going on and it's going to get worse before it gets better. Please, please, keep us safe and let them figure out who killed Steven before anything else happens.*

SIX

Clay rolled over and looked at the clock. Tuesday morning at three o'clock. He hoped all was well. Granny May had checked on him about an hour ago, and now he couldn't go back to sleep. He supposed that meant he didn't have a concussion. And even though he still had a headache, the worst of the pain had subsided.

He slid out of bed and much to his relief found he wasn't dizzy, just a little light-headed. And very thirsty. Probably from the pain medication.

On silent feet, he made his way to the kitchen. Granny May had been sure to point out the fact that she kept the refrigerator stocked for her guests and he was to help himself. He decided to do just that.

Two steps from the entry to the kitchen he stopped and sniffed.

Smoke?

Another guest who was awake and had decided to light up a cigarette? Surely not.

A floorboard creaked behind him and he turned. "Someone there?"

"Clay?" Sabrina's breathy whisper reached him from the shadows, and the tension that had threaded his shoulders eased a bit.

"What are you doing up?"

"I thought I smelled smoke."

"Same here."

They entered the kitchen. Sabrina flipped on the light and Clay squinted his eyes as a new shaft of pain split through his skull. He gasped and turned back toward the darkened hallway. As his eyes adjusted, he gazed into the den. Flames crawled up one of the long window curtains.

"Sabrina, quick, get a fire extinguisher."

She turned. "Oh, no!" She rushed to the kitchen pantry and threw open the door. She grabbed the large red canister and shoved it at him. "Here!"

He pulled the pin and bolted into the den, aimed the hose at the flame and squeezed the handle.

White foam spewed from the nozzle, and Clay held it until the fire was out. He set the extinguisher down and looked at Sabrina. "How did that happen?"

Light filtered in from the kitchen and her face worried him. Fear etched itself in deep lines near her eyes and mouth. "I don't know."

"We're blessed we were awake." He knelt in

front of the mess, charred curtain, burnt flooring and foam.

He shot her a warm look. "Can you hand me the poker from the fireplace?"

Sabrina did. "What is it?"

He used the steel poker to jab at something and then lifted it. A small metal can sat on the pointed end. "This."

"I don't understand." She stared at the mess, coughed on the smoke, then walked over to the window—and pushed it up without a sound. "Or maybe I do." Cold air rushed in, and she shivered. She shut the window just as easily and latched it. "It wasn't locked." She bit her lip and shook her head. "Which is very odd. This may be a small town, but Granny May still takes precautions and always keeps her doors and windows locked at night."

He didn't touch the window but looked at it. "I'm guessing someone lifted it, placed an accelerant and some cloth in the can, lit it and put it under the curtain."

She swallowed. "Then shut the window."

"Prints would be on the outside. I have a kit in my car." He froze. "My car."

"It's all right. Lance took care of it. It's parked in front of the diner so no one asks any questions about why you were here last night. Tonight." She rubbed her eyes. "Whichever night."

"We're perfectly well chaperoned by your grandmother and whoever else is staying here."

She gave him a small smile. A very sad smile. "I know. But it was just better that way."

He wondered if her reaction had anything to do with her mother's reputation. Of course it did.

"Everything all right in here?" A man in his early fifties, followed by a woman about the same age, entered the den and gasped. "What happened?"

Granny May stepped around them and gaped. "Oh, no! What happened?"

"Just a little fire," Clay said. "But it's all taken care of now. Granny May, you'll have to call your insurance company first thing."

"How did it start?" She coughed on the residual smoke that lingered and waved a hand in front of her face.

Clay exchanged a glance with Sabrina. She walked over to her grandmother and placed a hand on her arm. "Why don't we deal with this in the morning?" She glanced at the mantel clock. "Which is only a couple of hours away." In a smooth move, she ushered her grandmother and the other couple back to the other part of the house.

Clay pulled his phone from his pocket and woke the sheriff.

* * *

Sabrina sat on the edge of her bed until five-thirty, then got up to start preparing breakfast for the guests. In total, it was just the couple—Mr. and Mrs. Flemming, who were in town visiting their children and grandchildren—Granny May, Clay and herself.

Breakfast didn't need to be ready until seven-thirty, but her mind raced, making sleep impossible. As she put together the ingredients for the biscuits, she thought about last night. Who would want to set fire to her grandmother's home? Had she made someone mad? Well, her grandmother hadn't, but Sabrina probably had. She snorted. In her line of work, she made people mad all the time. Mostly parents who had their children removed from their home.

Had one of them decided to seek revenge?

She thought about Stan Prescott. Had he come after her as a result of what had happened last night?

She wiped her hands on the well-used apron and placed the biscuits under a heat lamp to help them rise faster.

"Need some help?"

She yelped and spun to see Clay in the doorway. Sabrina placed a hand over her racing heart. "You scared me to death."

He grinned. "Sorry."

"How's your head this morning?"

"Pounding pretty hard, but nothing I can't live with."

Sabrina reached into the cabinet above her and pulled down a bottle of ibuprofen. She tossed it to him and then filled a glass with orange juice.

When she handed him the drink, his fingers closed over hers. A sweet warmth traveled up her arm and into her cheeks. His eyes narrowed, and she saw him swallow before taking the glass from her hand and downing three of the little orange pills.

Whoa. Okay. So the attraction was definitely mutual. In an effort to catch her breath and steady her racing pulse, she turned to the refrigerator to remove the slab of ham. She grabbed the electric knife from the drawer near the sink, plugged it in and set it on the counter. "Did you wind up going back to sleep after the sheriff came to dust for fingerprints?"

"No. You?"

"No. Not really."

Silence descended. He moved next to her, unwrapped the ham and placed it on the cutting board.

"You don't have to do that," she protested.

He smiled. "I don't mind. Feels domestic."

She gave a spurt of laughter but couldn't help it

that her mind went to all sorts of crazy thoughts at that comment. "Right. Domestic." She paused and watched him from the corner of her eye while she pulled down juice and milk glasses. "Do you want to be…er…domesticated?"

Clay glanced up at her and cocked his head. A slow smile curved his lips. "If I met the right person, sure."

Their gazes held a moment longer before Sabrina decided she'd better get out of the kitchen before she got burned.

"Don't go."

She turned back. "Go?" She cleared her throat and lifted a brow, hoping she looked innocent. "I'm just going to get the napkins from the pantry."

He lifted his brow to match hers. "Oh. Okay. But the pantry is over there."

"I know that," she snapped, embarrassed. But she couldn't stop the small smile that tugged at her lips.

He laughed and turned back to the ham. A few more moments passed in silence. He finished slicing the ham, and she covered it with plastic wrap and placed it back in the refrigerator.

"Who will you have do the repairs in the den?"

"I don't know. Do you know someone who's trustworthy?"

"No, but I can ask around. My dad would know someone."

"Okay."

"What's your story, Sabrina?"

She stopped. "What do you mean?" He simply looked at her.

She sighed and looked away, trying to decide if she wanted to answer the question.

What else needed doing? The eggs for the omelets. She walked to the refrigerator and pulled out a dozen eggs. She knew she was procrastinating. Clay did, too. He let her take her time. She finally met his eyes. "Well, you know my mother's reputation."

"Yes."

"It's shaped my whole life."

"How?"

She shrugged. "I used to think if I was perfect, somehow my mom would find out and come back for me."

"How did that work out for you?"

"It didn't, of course."

"So you've lived here all your life?"

"No. I lived in Nashville for several years. I just came back to Wrangler's Corner a year ago."

"Nashville!"

"That shocks you?"

"I've lived in Nashville for the past ten years."

"I know." She gave a sad smile. "Steven told me. It's a big city. I got my degree in social work there."

"So why come home?"

The memories stung, but not as bad as they used to. And in a different way. She no longer missed Brian; she just couldn't believe she'd been so stupid. "Because my boyfriend was aspiring to be a country-music singer and decided we should live together instead of getting married. Apparently marriage would cramp his style."

He cringed. "Ouch."

"I finally saw him for who he was and realized I didn't like him very much. I broke up with him and moved home to help my grandmother."

He covered her hand with his. "I'm glad you did."

She swallowed hard. "Yeah. Me, too."

He squeezed her fingers. Heat crept into her cheeks. He pulled her toward him, eyes on hers. Was he going to kiss her?

Flustered, she cleared her throat and pulled away. "I, uh, better get back to, uh, breakfast."

He gave a slow smile. "I'll help."

Together they finished getting breakfast ready. When her grandmother came in at six-fifteen and realized the only thing she had to do was finish cooking, she hugged them both.

Sabrina patted her on the back. "I'm going to get ready for the day."

"Better work a nap in somewhere."

"I wish. Don't forget to call the insurance company," Sabrina reminded her.

"As if." She waved. "Go on—I know you two have things you have to do today."

Sabrina kissed her cheek and looked at Clay. "I'll give the Zellises a call and let them know we're coming."

"I'm going to run home and get ready. I'll be back."

Sabrina watched him go and wondered at the feelings that seemed to be developing between them.

And wondered at the wisdom of getting involved with the man whose uncle couldn't stand her very existence.

Sadness engulfed her. Falling for Clay would probably be one of the dumbest things she could do.

She just hoped her heart got the message.

Clay assured everyone he felt much better and was just fine to drive. He'd driven home, changed clothes and made it back to the B and B in less than forty minutes. "I didn't wreck or run over anyone. I'm fine to drive."

Lance solved the argument. "Not this time. Get in. We only need to take one car anyway. I'll bring you back here when we're done."

Clay conceded with a groan. He motioned for Sabrina to take the front passenger seat, then climbed in behind her. Lance started the car and backed out of the parking spot. "Now, you let me take care of this." He glanced in the rearview mirror and caught Clay's eyes.

Clay nodded. "I promise."

Fifteen minutes later, Lance pulled into the lower-income neighborhood. He maneuvered through the streets until he came to a small ranch-style house with more weeds than grass. A motorcycle and a twenty-year-old Honda sat under the metal carport at the end of the drive.

Lance parked on the curb.

The front door opened. A woman Clay knew to be in her early fifties but who looked ten years older stepped out onto the porch. Clay rolled his window down as Lance and Sabrina exited the car.

The woman's shoulders softened slightly when she spotted Sabrina. "Is my boy in trouble again? Where are the little ones? He was supposed to be watching out for them." She wrung her hands.

Sabrina paused. "They're in a home right now being cared for. As for Jordan, no, ma'am, at least not the kind of trouble you're thinking. If he's in trouble, I don't think it's of his making. Is he here?"

Mrs. Zellis crossed her arms. "No, he ain't."

Sabrina frowned. "He called me yesterday and said he was scared." She debated whether to mention the fact that someone had taken a shot at her yesterday. She decided not to for the moment.

"You know he's not really very happy staying

here." She shrugged. "He's seventeen years old. Be eighteen next week. I can only do what I can do."

Clay figured the woman was right. If a seventeen-year-old boy didn't want to stay with his grandmother and he had a way to get his hands on some cash and a place to sleep at night, then his grandmother was pretty powerless.

"I don't think Jordan's not here because he doesn't want to be. I think he's afraid and is hiding from someone," Sabrina said.

"Probably one of those people he hangs out with turned on him. I told him he couldn't trust them none."

Sabrina moved closer but stopped at the bottom of the porch steps. "When was the last time you saw him?"

The woman sucked her teeth, then pooched her lips out. She let her gaze drop from Sabrina's. Clay wanted to jump from the car and shake the information from her. Instead he clenched his fingers into fists and waited.

"Mrs. Zellis?" Sabrina pushed.

She sighed. "Nigh on two or three days, I reckon. His mama left last week, so it's just been me and the kids." She paused. "They all right? I saw you tried to call last night. I didn't worry too much because I figured they were with Jordan, but you're saying they're not."

"They're fine. They're in a foster home for now."

She nodded and tears welled before she blinked them away. "Might be best if they stay there for now."

Sabrina nodded. "If Jordan comes home, will you have him call me?"

"Sure. But you know how he knows these mountains like the back of his hand. If he doesn't want to be found, he won't be. He likes the caves up there." She gave an absent nod in the direction of the mountains.

Sabrina looked at Lance. He sighed and shook his head. "I'll file a report. We'll get his picture out there and get people looking for him." He wrote in his little green notebook, then tapped the pencil against his chin. "Do you know if Jordan ever spoke to Deputy Steven Starke a few weeks ago?"

"Starke?" Her brow wrinkled. "Ain't that the cop who got hisself killed?"

"Yes, ma'am."

"No. Jordan never said anything about him." She paused, her forehead still wrinkled. "Wait a second. I think that deputy did come out here and ask to see Jordan. I thought the boy was here, but he never came out when I called to him. That deputy left his number, but I don't think Jordan ever called him."

"Do you know why Deputy Starke wanted to talk to Jordan?" Lance asked.

"No." She fidgeted with the hem of her ratty T-shirt.

"If you were to go looking for Jordan, where would you look?" Sabrina asked.

Mrs. Zellis didn't hesitate. "Told you. Those caves. Or at that old abandoned mill across the county line. A bunch of them teenagers go out there to party and the like. I'm sure that's where Jordy's probably got to."

Clay figured she was probably right. He kept his ear to the crack in the window, not wanting to miss a word.

"I saw him."

Clay lifted his gaze to see Mr. Zellis come into view.

"Saw who, sir?" Lance asked.

"The cop. When he came out to find Jordan."

Clay tensed. Lance didn't change his relaxed stance. "Is that right? What'd you see?"

"Deputy Starke. He'd been out here several times, so I knew it was him. He came to the house and when he didn't find Jordan, he left. As he was leaving, Jordan and his buddy came out of the workshop over there and followed him."

"So Steven and Jordan *did* talk." Sabrina clasped her hands in front of her.

"Yes. All three of them did. And there was

another car, too. Parked in the neighbor's drive. It followed the deputy and the boys."

"Who was the other boy with Jordan?" Lance asked, shifting his notebook to his other hand.

"That Trey Wilde kid."

Lance blinked and rubbed his chin. He turned slightly and exchanged a glance with Clay. Clay silently urged him on. "What kind of car?" Lance asked.

"A dark blue or black sedan. Not sure the make or model."

"And it wasn't your neighbor's car?"

"Nope. He's got a pickup he takes to work. Single guy who lives alone and only has one vehicle. That's the reason I noticed the sedan."

Frustration mingled with excitement inside Clay. Why hadn't someone found this out shortly after Steven's death?

"Did you tell the sheriff about this?" Sabrina asked.

"Nope." He shrugged. "No one asked."

And he couldn't be bothered to come forward and volunteer the information. Clay wanted to slug him. Instead he drew in a deep breath, trying to slow the adrenaline zipping through his veins.

"All right, then. Can you think of anything else that might be helpful before we leave?" Lance asked.

"Nope."

"You're sure?"

"I'm sure." The man turned and disappeared in the direction he'd come from.

His wife started to shut the door, and Sabrina stopped her. "Is Jordan's camera here? When he called me yesterday, he said he was taking pictures."

"It's not here. If he's not in the house, that camera ain't either, but I'll look." She shut the door.

Clay fidgeted. Why was she asking about that camera?

About a minute later, the woman opened the door again. "It's not here. Didn't figure it would be."

Sabrina nodded. "Okay. Thanks."

She and Lance headed back to the car. As soon as they were in their seats, Clay said, "We just have to work with what we have. I remember that place across the county line. Can't believe it's still standing."

"It's still there," Lance said.

"Then let's head out there."

Lance hesitated. "Look, Clay—"

"Were you and Steven friends or not?"

"Yes. We were. Everyone on the force was friends with Steven." The deputy's quiet words echoed in the car.

"I know you don't want me along, but I promise I won't do anything to jeopardize this investigation. This is my brother we're talking about, and I know what could happen if I mess up."

"Yes, like evidence getting thrown out, me getting fired for letting you come along, shall I go on?"

"I'm not going to take that chance. I just want to ride, to be there. I did fine just now, right? Never left the car."

Lance leaned his head back and closed his eyes. "Ned's going to kill me if he finds out about this."

"Nothing for him to get upset about. I'm not investigating."

"Right. You're not investigating." Lance cranked the car and pulled away from the Zellis home.

"So where to first?" Clay asked. "You want to visit the Wilde home or the abandoned, yet occupied, mill?"

Lance's radio crackled. He responded, and Clay sighed when the man said, "I gotta go."

"I heard."

"Don't do anything stupid," Lance said with a resigned expression.

"Wouldn't think of it."

SEVEN

"You're going to do something stupid, aren't you?" Sabrina asked after Lance dropped them back at the bed-and-breakfast. Clay shot her an innocent look she didn't believe for a minute. She nodded. "All right, then. Let's go."

"Where?"

"Wherever it is you plan to go. You're either going to the mill or the caves, aren't you?"

Clay's jaw worked as though he was trying to figure out whether he should admit it or not. He finally said, "Yes, I want to go scout around the caves. I'm like you. The longer Jordan stays gone, the more worried I am something's going to happen to him."

"Let me change and call my boss. I'll tell her I'm going to look for Jordan."

"You don't have to go."

She gave him a sad smile. "Yes, I do. Jordan reached out to me for help. I'm going to do my best to give it to him." Grief flashed in Clay's eyes.

Concerned, Sabrina laid a hand on his arm. "What is it, Clay?"

He cleared his throat. "Steven asked me for help and I didn't give it to him."

"You had no way of knowing he would get killed."

Clay nodded. "Right." He walked to his cruiser, and she followed to climb in the passenger seat.

"I guess you know where the caves are," she said.

"I do."

"Been there a few times in your youth?"

A hint of a smile played on his lips. "A few times. You?"

"Me? Never." The smile flipped and he gave her a questioning look. She shrugged. "That wouldn't have been the smart thing to do. The kids who went to the caves were the wild ones, the ones looking for trouble. Me? All I wanted was to be liked. And to be perfect. If I went to the caves, people would have talked." She shook her head. "They were just waiting for me to turn out like my mother. I was just as determined to prove them wrong."

He reached over and squeezed her fingers. "It wasn't easy growing up in this town, was it?"

"No. It wasn't easy."

Clay fell silent and she was glad. She didn't want to talk about her mother or the emotional scars the woman had left on her. She did pray her mother had found some peace and that if she was dead, that she'd found God before she died. If she was alive...well, that was a thought for another day.

Sabrina reached her boss, and the woman told her to be careful. "Keep me updated."

"I will."

She hung up. "Has anyone found Trey Wilde?" she asked Clay.

"Nope. Ned called to ask about him. His father said he'd gone to do a college visit with his mother and hadn't gotten home yet."

Sabrina frowned. "In the middle of the week? Missing school?"

Clay glanced at her. "That does sound kind of odd, doesn't it?"

"Then again, this is the Wilde family we're talking about. 'Kind of odd' is a good description. They're extremely private. They have bodyguards and security like something you would only expect to find with celebrities or something."

"Why all the heavy armor?"

"They're rich. I suppose that can make someone a little paranoid."

"I suppose." His frown remained and she could almost hear his wheels turning.

"I want to talk to Mr. Wilde. If Trey has a bodyguard, maybe the guy saw something the day he and Jordan talked to Steven." He shook his head.

"Well, rumor has it that the elder Mr. Wilde is

often furious with Trey for giving his bodyguards the slip."

"Oh."

"Yeah." She bit her lip. "Do you want to go there first?"

"Just show up? You think he'd see us?"

"Maybe. It's worth a try, don't you think?"

He gave a slow nod, then cut her a glance. "You're not trying to keep me from going up to the caves, are you?"

Sabrina widened her eyes. "Would I do that?"

He grunted, but she thought she caught a slight smile tip the corners of his mouth.

She pulled Trey's address up on her phone and directed him to the affluent area on the edge of Wrangler's Corner.

The security guard in the brick guardhouse stepped out to greet them as Clay pulled to a stop. "May I help you?"

Clay flashed his badge. "Would Mr. Wilde be willing to talk to us about his son?"

A small frown appeared on the man's face. "Let me call." After a brief wait, the guard opened the gate. "He'll be waiting for you."

"Thanks." He looked at Sabrina after he rolled the window up. "Why do I feel like that was just too easy?"

She frowned. "I know."

Clay drove up the winding drive to park at the

top of the concrete horseshoe. The door opened and a tall man with a military buzz cut held out a hand. "IDs?"

Sabrina raised a brow and pulled out her wallet. Clay flashed his badge. "The uniform doesn't speak for itself?"

After an intense scrutiny of the plastic, the man handed Sabrina her license back and gave a clipped nod. "Follow me." He led them into a den area. "Have a seat. Mr. Wilde will be with you shortly."

Sabrina sat on the sofa, and Clay lowered himself next to her. She swallowed at the sudden jump in her pulse. Her awareness of him wasn't going away. Instead it seemed to be growing exponentially with each moment she spent in his presence.

"Nice place," Clay said.

"That's an understatement." The Oriental rug, leather furniture, high-end entertainment center and the Waterford crystal shouted affluence. "But all that money hasn't kept his son out of trouble."

"Good point."

He didn't keep them waiting. Mr. Wilde entered the room with the air of a man used to being in charge. Clay stood, as did Sabrina. The three exchanged handshakes. "Thanks for seeing us, Mr. Wilde."

"What's this about?"

His abrupt attitude rubbed Sabrina the wrong way, but she kept silent and let Clay take the lead.

"We'd like to speak with Trey, but I understand he's with your wife visiting colleges."

Something flashed across the man's face. Something subtle and almost not there, but Sabrina caught it. "What is it?"

"Nothing."

"No, there's something. He's not with your wife, is he?"

"Of course he is."

"Could I have her phone number, then? I'd like to talk to her."

The man's eyes narrowed. "You're going to call her?"

"Yes. Is there some reason I shouldn't?"

His shoulders slumped. His arrogance and haughtiness fell from him like a landslide. "Then you'll find out, I suppose."

"Find out what?"

He hesitated. Fear flickered in his eyes. "I hate to admit it, but I don't know where Trey is and I'm starting to get worried."

"What do you mean?" Sabrina asked.

"I mean he's been gone for weeks. I heard him leave one night and he never came back."

"Why haven't you reported this?" Clay's shout rang through the room.

Sabrina laid a hand on his arm. To Mr. Wilde she said, "You didn't report him missing because you don't think he's missing. You think he just left."

Mr. Wilde nodded. "He's constantly telling me how much he hates it here. He refused the bodyguards, threatened to have them arrested for harassment, stalking, whatever he could think of. I told them to back off, but Trey..." He shrugged. "Trey had had enough, I guess. He won't answer his phone—in fact, it goes straight to voice mail. He hasn't called, nothing. I thought if I gave him some space, he'd come around."

"What's his relationship like with his mother?" Clay asked.

"They get along all right." He frowned. "It does concern me a bit that he hasn't at least called her."

Clay nodded. "Why did you lie? Make up a story about where he was?"

The man pulled in a deep breath and dropped his eyes.

"Because he didn't want anyone to know he'd left," Sabrina said. "Am I right?"

"Yes. I hired a private detective to find him, but even he came up empty." He pinched the bridge of his nose. "Trey had plenty of cash handy. He's not using his credit cards." He shrugged. "Or mine, so..."

"So you come clean now with us because you've been confronted. How long would you have waited if we hadn't pushed for the information?" The steel in Clay's voice told Sabrina what he thought about this man as a father.

Mr. Wilde lifted his chin and narrowed his eyes. "You don't know anything about Trey so don't judge me."

Sabrina cleared her throat. Clay gave a short nod. "Until Trey decides to surface, we might be at a dead end," Clay said.

"Yes."

"I'll put a BOLO out on him. We need to find him."

"What's the urgency?" Mr. Wilde asked.

"Your son was seen with Jordan Zellis."

He stiffened. "That scum? When?"

"He's not scum, sir. He's a young man who needs guidance. He's also missing and we're thinking he and Trey are together." Sabrina refused to sit there and let him malign Jordan.

Mr. Wilde ignored her and kept his gaze on Clay. "When?"

"The day Deputy Steven Starke was killed. We have an eyewitness who puts Trey and Jordan with Deputy Starke." Clay held up a hand. "And just to be clear, I'm not investigating the death of Deputy Starke. I'm simply looking for two missing boys."

The man's eyes narrowed. "Right."

"If you hear from Trey, will you let us know?"

"Of course. Joseph will show you out." And with that, he turned on his heel and left the room.

A minute later, they were seated in Clay's cruiser.

"I have so much going on in my brain, I'm dizzy," Sabrina muttered.

"Ditto."

"So what now? The caves?"

"Works for me."

As Clay drove, they fell into a comfortable silence, but her nerves still jumped. She couldn't help watching her rearview mirror. She hadn't forgotten someone had taken a shot at her just yesterday. "You know, I haven't really thought about this, but after all that's happened, I'm wondering if they're connected."

"If what's connected?"

"The day of Steven's funeral, I left the graveside and on my way home, I was almost run off the side of the mountain."

"What?" He frowned. "What happened?"

"Just what I said. I thought at first the driver was just being careless, trying to pass me on a double yellow line, so I slowed down. When I did, he moved over and forced me off the road."

"Did he actually hit you?"

"He bumped me. Fortunately, I was going as slow as I was and I was able to stop on the edge. He raced on past me. The car behind me stopped and asked if I was all right."

"Did you report it?"

"Sure, but I didn't get a license number. I described the vehicle to Ned. He knew a couple of people who had trucks like that and investigated, but none of the trucks had any damage to indicate a collision."

Clay drew his eyebrows together. "Anything after that?"

"Not as blatant as that. But I've often felt like I've been watched in the weeks since Steven's death. It's been creepy. But with this crazy stuff of being lured out to a trailer and getting shot at, someone following me from the diner, then attacking you, my grandmother's home being set on fire—" She shook her head. "It just makes me wonder if it's all related."

"That's a good question."

The mountain road wound up for about a mile. The ride didn't take long and soon Clay parked the cruiser in the small clearing. "On the weekends, this place is packed," she said. "It's weird to see it so empty."

"I know. I've had to patrol it several times since I've been back. Broke up two fights, hauled kids in for underage drinking." He sighed. "I can't believe the county hasn't shut this place down. Bulldozed it or something. Sure would save the deputies quite a bit of trouble."

"I don't know," Sabrina said as she climbed from the car. "If kids are going to get in trouble, they'll find a way."

"True enough. Let's just hope we can find Jordan and Trey before they get themselves in so much trouble, they can't find their way out."

Clay looked around, shivering even while his senses tingled. Memories flooded him, but he pushed them aside. "You'd think the stories about people getting hurt would keep others away from these caves."

"I think that just entices some people," Sabrina said. The air felt thin on top of the mountain. Clay grabbed the flashlight from his glove compartment and walked toward the nearest cave. He braced himself for the fact that it would be even colder inside.

The three caves brought back the flood of memories once again. As a teen, he'd done the same as the young people today and gone exploring in the yawning black holes. He stepped inside the nearest one and listened. Nothing except an echoing silence and the pounding of his own heartbeat.

The temperature dropped a good ten degrees as he walked farther from the entrance. Clay kicked aside beer and soda cans and fast-food wrappers. Jordan's? Or left over from the weekend of partying teens?

He felt Sabrina's presence behind him. "I don't think he's staying in this one, if he's even here," he said.

"How would we even know? His trash would blend right in."

"Unfortunately."

"Want to check the other two?"

"Sure."

The second and third caves yielded nothing, either. Sabrina's shoulders drooped. "I was so sure he'd be here."

"We still have one more place to look."

"The abandoned mill?"

"Yep."

Clay led her back into the sunlight, squinting at the brightness.

A sharp crack sounded. Sabrina cried out and dropped.

"Sabrina!" His mind registered the gunshot even as he bent and grabbed her from the hard ground. He ducked back into the cave, moving fast and carrying her deep inside. He stopped only when the light from the opening dimmed and he couldn't go any farther without risking tripping. He set her on the floor as he reached for his weapon with one hand, his phone with the other. "Be still, okay? I don't know how bad you're hurt."

She groaned and lifted a hand to her left shoulder. "He shot me. Somebody shot me." He heard the shock in her words.

"Yeah." Clay dialed 911. And the call dropped. Inside the cave, he wasn't going to be able to get a signal. Fear and frustration pounded through him. Not just for himself but for Sabrina. How bad had she been hit?

She stared at her right hand now covered in blood. He gingerly pulled her jacket off, almost unable to bear the sound of her sharp gasp. He knew it hurt. Now he needed to be able to see.

He'd dropped the flashlight at the entrance. He improvised and used his phone to see the wound on her shoulder. The flashlight app lit up the cave. He just hoped no one had decided to come after them inside the cave. "Your pretty coat and sweater are done for, I'm afraid."

She gave a half laugh, half groan. "I'm okay with losing those. I can replace them. How bad does my shoulder look?"

He poked as gently as he could. She still flinched, but he got a good look at the wound. "Actually, it doesn't look too bad. The bullet grazed you."

"That's twice now he's shot and missed." She glanced down and tears fell from her eyes. She sniffed, blinked and looked back at him. "I'm afraid if there's a third time, he just might succeed."

Clay winced. "I'm not sure I'd call this one a miss."

"I'm still alive. I'm counting it as a miss."

"I'll go with that." He didn't want to think about

her dying. "I have a first-aid kit in the car. I just have to get to it."

With her good hand, she grabbed his forearm. "No, you can't go out there."

He held up his cell. "I'm not getting a signal in here. We need help, and we need it fast."

"What if he's out there waiting? He'll just shoot you as soon as you stick your head outside."

A scraping sound at the entrance made him tense. Sabrina froze, but he could hear her breathing in tight, pained pants. "Stay put," he whispered.

Clay scuttled back toward the entrance, his weapon held in front of him. Enough sunlight shone through, enabling him to see well enough to walk, to see shadows.

A figure darted in front of the entrance.

"Police! Identify yourself!"

The individual fired off another round that slammed into the cave above his head. Clay aimed and pulled the trigger.

His ears rang, and he ducked back. Heard running feet. Clay dashed out, squinting against the sun, willing his eyes to adjust fast.

By the time he could see well enough, a dark figure wearing a motorcycle helmet was roaring down the mountainside.

Clay whipped out his phone. This time the call to 911 went through.

When he finished the call, he raced back to

Sabrina's side and found her with her head against the wall of the cave, lips moving silently. "You praying?"

She looked at him. "It's about the only thing I know to do."

He held a hand out for her. "Help's on the way."

She sighed and let him help her to her feet. He gripped her good arm and she sagged against him before gaining her footing. "Sorry."

Instead of setting her from him, he wrapped her in a hug and held her. She stiffened, then relaxed. And Clay just held her until they heard help arrive.

EIGHT

Sabrina found herself back at the hospital. Only this time she was the patient, and she wasn't happy about it. The doctor shook her head. "It's really just a scratch. It could be a lot worse."

Sabrina shot her a dark look. "I've had a scratch before. This isn't anything like what I remember a scratch feeling like." She softened. "I'm sorry. I'm grumpy and scared, but I know what you mean. Thanks."

Rachel patted her hand. "You ready for a visitor?"

"Sure."

Thirty seconds later, Clay stepped into the room. "You okay?"

"I'm fine. It's just a scratch." She looked at him—really looked at him—and felt her heart thump a little faster. He'd been so amazing through everything. When he'd held her in the cave, she'd immediately felt better. Comforted. Still scared out of her mind, true. But being in his arms had allowed her to hold on to her sanity. "I don't know what I would have done without you today, Clay."

He touched her cheek with his forefinger, then tucked his hands into his front pockets. "Well, I don't think you would have been out in the caves if I hadn't taken you there."

She sighed. "Well, that's true. Then again, who knows? This person seems determined to come after me and I have no idea what I've done to make someone want to kill me."

He paced from one end of the small room to the other. "I've been thinking about that."

"Do you have an answer?"

"It has to have something to do with Steven. Someone thinks you either have something or know something about his death."

"But I don't."

"What if you do and you just don't know you do?"

She blinked. "Okay. But what? How do I figure that out?"

He sat in the chair next to the bed. "Think back to your times with Steven. What did you talk about? Where did you meet? Did he give you anything?"

She leaned her head back against the pillow and stared at the ceiling. "We met once or twice a week. He was often the deputy on duty when I had to make a home visit or pick up children from abusive situations, so we became pretty good friends. We talked about a lot of things." She gave a small smile. "Mostly books."

"Ah, yes, my brother the bibliophile. Were you guys more than friends?" he asked, his voice soft, hesitant.

She met his gaze. "No. We both love to read. Anything and everything. Mostly mysteries or books on theology. We'd read a book and discuss it. Sometimes I'd read a book and give it to him thinking he'd enjoy it and he'd do the same for me, but romance never entered the picture. I think Steven was still grieving Misty."

"Yeah." Clay cleared his throat. "He was."

"He talked about her a lot. He also talked about your parents a good bit and about your mother's remission from breast cancer."

"It'll be five years in January." He rubbed his eyes. "That was a rough time."

"He was so stressed that he couldn't help them more financially."

"Financially? Why would he need to do that?"

She froze, then picked at the bedspread with her good hand. He covered it with his. "What else, Sabrina?"

"You don't know." It wasn't a question and she knew she'd just put her foot in her mouth. "I assumed you did."

"Know what?" His quiet question echoed in the room as though he'd shouted it.

Sabrina sighed. "He...ah...he mentioned the financial difficulties your parents were having and said that was one reason they wanted to take in foster kids."

Clay jerked back and she missed the warmth of his hand. "Financial difficulties? What are you talking about?"

"You really don't know?"

"Obviously not."

She bit her lip. "I don't want to gossip."

"It's not gossip—it's my family." A muscle ticked in the side of his jaw. "Tell me. Please."

"You mother's cancer nearly wiped them out financially. They've been close to losing the farm."

Clay stood. "I knew the medical bills were bad, but I thought— Who else knows? I mean besides Steven, who can't do anything about it now."

She flinched at his sarcasm. "I don't know. From what I understand, your parents didn't want to worry you guys, but they finally broke down and told Steven so they wouldn't lose the farm and because he had a right to know what he was going to be inheriting."

Clay stopped and stared out the window. "Will you be all right for a little while?"

"Of course."

"I'll ask Ned if he has a deputy or someone who can come watch your room."

"Where are you going?"

"To have a long-overdue talk with my parents."

Clay got on the phone with Ned and requested a deputy stay with Sabrina. "And can you put someone on the B and B? I've got a personal item to take care of."

"Everything all right, son?"

"That's what I'm going to find out."

Clay waited until Lance Goode arrived. He relaxed a fraction. Lance hitched his belt and finished off the soda he'd been drinking. He tossed the can in the recycle bin. "What's up? Ned said you needed someone to watch out for Sabrina."

"Yeah." He told his friend everything that had happened up near the caves. "Ned called a forensics team from Nashville to come see if they could find anything. If we could find some bullet casings, at least we'd have a type of weapon. I'm pretty sure it's a rifle."

"You think Prescott's the one shooting?"

"He's my first choice. His home has been confiscated and is being cleaned up by a crew. You know Stan. Where would he go?"

Lance shook his head. "We've looked in all of

the places we thought he might run to, but he hasn't shown his face. No sign of the kid, either."

"But we're getting shot at," Clay muttered. "Why?"

Lance sighed. "Go do your errand. I'll take care of your lady."

"My lady?" Clay asked.

"Isn't she?"

Clay cocked his head, thoughtful. "Not yet."

Lance laughed. "Soon enough, then."

"If I can keep her alive." They both sobered. "Thanks. I'll text you when I'm on my way back. I think she's staying overnight."

"You need me to take a shift with you? Krissy's staying with her mom this weekend. We're forgoing the concert. Her brother called and he had something come up at work."

Krissy, Lance's wife, was taking turns with her brother caring for their mother, who suffered from Alzheimer's. Still in the beginning stages of the condition, she could stay in her home but couldn't be alone. "How's her mom doing?"

Lance's jaw tightened. "It's a horrible disease. And an expensive one."

"I'm sorry."

"Yeah, me, too. And you don't have any idea how mad she is about missing that concert. I'll be happy to take an extra shift."

Clay clapped his friend's forearm. "I'll let you know if I need you."

Clay left Lance parked outside of Sabrina's door and hurried to the elevator.

Fifteen minutes later, he walked in his parents' back door.

And did a double take.

His brother Seth sat on the couch, the remote to the television in his right hand. Encased in plaster from foot to thigh, his left leg rested on the cushions.

"What happened to you?"

"A mean ole bull and a belly roll."

Clay cringed. A belly roll meant the bull had come completely off the ground, kicking and twisting to the side in a rolling motion. Only the best managed to stay on for the required eight seconds. And Seth was one of the best. "What distracted you?"

Seth jerked. "No one."

"No *one?*" Now, that was an interesting comment. "Who is she?"

A darkness he'd never seen before came over Seth's face. "Drop it. What do you want?"

Clay considered pushing the topic with his younger brother, but the look in the man's eyes said he'd better not. "Where's Dad?"

"Out with the horses. Someone bought Nightshade and is coming by to get him."

"Nightshade? That's one of Dad's favorite horses."

Seth frowned. "I know. Seems weird he'd sell him, but when I asked, Dad just shook his head and muttered for me not to worry about it."

So Seth didn't know about the financial issues. Clay wouldn't say anything until he'd talked with his dad. "Thanks."

"Yeah." Seth picked up the remote and flipped the channel.

Knowing his parents were in danger of losing the home he'd grown up in made him look at the place with fresh eyes. It needed work. A fresh coat of paint, the hardwoods sanded and refinished, the furniture repaired or replaced. All of it. He hadn't really noticed it before now. To him it was just home.

His phone rang as he walked toward the barn. Lance. "What's up?"

"They're releasing Sabrina."

"What? So soon?"

"Doc says she can go. She's signing the papers now."

Clay stopped and thought. "She can't go back to the B and B—she's too accessible."

"Well, she's rolling out of here in about ten minutes."

"Bring her here."

"You're sure?"

"Yes. And watch your back. The person after her doesn't care who gets in the way."

"I'll be careful. See you in about thirty minutes."

Clay hung up and found his father in the barn brushing down the horse he'd just sold. "Why didn't you tell me?" he asked.

His father looked at him. "Tell you what, son?"

"That you're in trouble financially."

His father stilled. "What are you talking about?"

"You know what I'm talking about."

"Who told you?"

"Steven. Indirectly." He didn't want to mention Sabrina as his source, not with tension about her so high, but he didn't want to lie, either.

"Indirectly."

"Yeah." His father resumed his rhythmic brushing. Clay stroked the animal's velvety nose. "You can't sell Nightshade."

"I can and I did." His dad cleared his throat. "And I'd rather not talk about it."

"How much money are you talking about?"

A sigh slipped from the man's lips. He closed his eyes. "You're not going to let this go, are you?"

"Nope."

"A quarter of a million."

Clay swallowed. "Wow."

Silence descended for a brief moment. Then Clay snagged the pick from the bucket. He nudged the horse's leg and started working on the hoof, digging out the packed-in dirt and other debris. "And you only told Steven. Why keep it from the rest of us?"

"Because you kids couldn't do anything about it. No sense in worrying you." He shrugged. "I had to let Steven know where we were financially because he wanted the ranch. He loved being a cop, but his heart was the ranch."

"Yeah. I know." He finished the last hoof, then put the pick down and straightened. "Fostering kids isn't going to bring in the kind of money you need to keep this place going."

His dad finally looked at him. A small sad smile played on his lips. "Nope, but it keeps your mom busy and gives her someone to grandmother."

"Ah."

"Her cancer treatments sent us into a financial mess we've never been able to clean up. The insurance didn't cover much. I mortgaged the farm to the hilt, and now I'm barely making the payments. The only reason we still have the place is because Frank Banner is my best friend."

Frank Banner, owner of Wrangler's Corner's one and only family-owned bank.

"I see."

"But even Frank can't give me infinite extensions."

"Right." He paused. "We found Steven's wallet."

His father flinched. "What?"

"Ned's investigating. Looks like someone took it from him when he was killed. We found it in a trailer on the outskirts of town."

"We? Who's we? And what trailer?" His father's voice had thickened.

"Doesn't matter. When this is all over, Mom will have it."

His dad sniffed. "She was going through some of his things just this morning. She has a special box, you know. One where she keeps everything he had on him at the time he died. The coroner gave them to us when we went to…ah…see him." His dad coughed and his eyes reddened. "She keeps those along with a lot of his baby items. And his wedding ring." Clay reached out to squeeze his father's shoulder. "This morning she was just sitting on the bed crying, cradling each of the objects as though they were Steven himself."

Clay's throat tightened. Before he could think of words that might offer comfort, he heard a car pull up on the gravel drive outside the barn. He figured Lance and Sabrina had arrived. He turned back to his father and cleared his throat. "I have a favor to ask."

"Name it."

"Can Sabrina stay here at the house?" The silence felt thick and Clay almost wanted to squirm. He resisted. "She's in danger, Dad. I don't want her alone."

"Your uncle would have a fit."

"Uncle Abe needs to grow a heart."

His father leveled him a steely stare. "Her mother is the reason his heart is hard as a rock. It broke in half, then froze that way."

Clay sighed. "I know, but this is your house, your land, not his. Will you do this for me? For her?" Still his father didn't answer, and Clay wanted to growl with frustration. "I've never known you not to do the right thing. Let the past stay in the past. She needs help, so help her."

"Fine!" His father threw his hands in the air in surrender. "Fine. She can stay here, but she can't stay at the house. Let her take your cottage. You can stay at the house. And if Abe comes by, she needs to make sure she makes herself scarce."

"The house would be safer, Dad."

His father's eyes hardened. "The cottage. If she's got danger following her, I don't want it around your mother."

Clay nodded. "I understand. I don't plan to let danger get that close to her, but thanks. I'll let her know."

He left his father to his horses and went to meet Sabrina and Lance. She smiled when she saw him, but she couldn't hide the confusion in her eyes. He helped her from the car. He looked at Lance. "Thanks. Anyone follow you?"

"Not that I saw."

"What's going on? Why did he bring me here?" Sabrina asked.

"What do you think about staying here for a while?"

She furrowed her brow. "Here? Where?"

"I originally wanted you in the house with the family. But my father said no. He's worried Abe will come by and find you there." He frowned. "I've never known my father to care what his brother thought. This is very out of character for him." He shook his head. "But you can stay at my place. I'll move into the house and be nearby if you need something."

She shook her head before he even finished speaking. "I can't. I mean, think of the imposition." She cradled her wounded arm. "I don't think so."

"You can stay."

Clay turned to find his father standing in the doorway of the barn. The man's gruff exterior covered a heart as soft as a marshmallow. He knew this. He'd grown up with it. The hard shell and the soft interior. So his father's determination to let Abe dictate how he ran his house bothered him. His father's gaze locked on her arm in the sling. He shook his head. "Shooting a woman. Ridiculous," he muttered.

Clay's phone vibrated, and he pulled it from his pocket. Before he answered, he looked hard at

Sabrina. "Please stay." The he checked the caller ID. "Excuse me." He lifted the phone to his ear. "Starke here."

"We got him." Ned's voice rumbled with satisfaction.

"Prescott?"

"Yep. He'd stolen a chicken from the Harris farm and was cooking it down by the river when two hikers came across him. He didn't see them, but they saw him and recognized him. We nabbed him just as he finished his dinner."

"Good, then the county doesn't have to waste money feeding him," Clay said. He glanced over at Sabrina and Lance. Sabrina had her phone to her ear, her expression dark as a thundercloud.

Ned snorted. "Right. We've booked him and are holding him."

"I want to talk to him."

"Now, Clay, you know I can't let you do that."

"Then I want to listen in when you question him. Please."

Ned's loud sigh made Clay tense. If the man said no...

"All right, but you stay out of sight."

"Thanks."

Sabrina was still on her phone, her hand pressed to her head.

"Can you be here in about two hours?"

Sabrina hung up and paced from one end of the

car to the other. Lance placed a hand on her shoulder and Clay straightened.

"Clay? You there?"

"I'm here. You said two hours. I'll be there." He hung up. "Good news."

Sabrina turned, her eyes fiery. "Actually, bad news."

"What are you talking about?"

"Someone just broke into my grandmother's house and trashed the office."

NINE

Sabrina wondered if her muscles would ever relax again. Her grandmother had assured her she was fine.

"What happened?" Clay asked as he helped Sabrina into the front seat of his cruiser. Lance had already taken off toward the B and B.

"Granny May had gone to the grocery store. Her boarders were gone doing whatever they do and when she got home, someone had gone in and wrecked the office."

"How did they get in?"

"The door is unlocked during the day. Whoever did it just walked right in and helped themselves."

"Was anything stolen?"

"Not that she can see."

Fear for her grandmother curled in her belly. What had she done to bring this down on the only family she had?

When they pulled into the parking area of the B and B, Ned stood by his cruiser talking into his radio. Lance had parked himself on the front porch and Granny May huddled in her heavy down coat looking lost and alone. And mad.

Sabrina launched herself from the vehicle as soon as Clay came to a stop. "Are you all right?" She raced up the front steps and hugged her with her good arm. "Let's go inside."

"What happened to you?" Her grandmother touched Sabrina's wounded arm.

Sabrina winced. There was no way she could keep her grandmother out of the loop now. She needed to know everything. "Someone tried to kill me today, Granny May."

The poor woman shook like a leaf in the wind. "Oh, me. Oh, dear me."

Sabrina's heart tightened. She couldn't remember ever seeing the woman so upset. She led her inside and seated her on the couch in the living area. Clasping her grandmother's cold hands in hers, she asked, "Did you notice anything stolen?"

"No. Nothing." She gave a shrug. "But I was only able to do a quick glance before they made me leave. It appears that was the only room that was disturbed. What do you mean, someone tried to kill you?"

"Someone shot at me today. Thankfully, the bullet only grazed me."

"Why would someone shoot at you, Brina?" Disbelief shone in her grandmother's eyes.

"We don't know. Clay was with me, and we think it may have something to do with Steven's death."

Granny May gaped. "I don't even know what to think."

"I know. I don't, either." Sabrina looked around. "But I know one thing. You're going to have to start locking the door when you leave."

"But how will the guests get in?"

"We'll get a lock with a code. You can give your guests the code."

"And change it every week," Clay said from the doorway.

Sabrina stood as Ned appeared behind him. "I want to see the office."

Ned nodded. Clay motioned for her to follow him. "I'll be right back," she told her grandmother.

Clay took some blue booties from Ned. "We're going to do this right." He slipped the booties on his shoes, and Sabrina did the same. Next, the gloves. She shook her head as he helped her slide her uninjured hand into one. Her grandmother's house was a crime scene. Again. It was all too surreal.

From the living area, she turned left to walk down the hallway past the stairs and into the first room on the right. Besides her bedroom, Sabrina loved this room the most.

Or she had.

She'd prepared herself for it to be bad, but this was— "Oh...wow."

Books pulled from the floor-to-ceiling shelves, the sofa upended, one of the lamps thrown on the floor—and it looked as if someone had had a temper tantrum on top of it. Drawers had been yanked from her grandfather's antique desk and dumped, the contents strewn from one end of the office to the other.

The laptop lay in the middle of the floor. Even one of the curtains had been pulled from the window. Sabrina blinked hard as tears raced to the surface.

An arm slid across her shoulders. She knew it was Clay, and she wanted nothing more than to lean into his strength and cry out her anger. Instead she sucked in a deep breath. "Who would do this? Why?"

"Looks like they were searching for something."

She gave a slow nod. "You think that's why they're trying to kill me? Because they think I have something or know something related to Steven's death and they want to make sure I don't...what? Talk about it? Surely they know if I knew or had something, I would have already told or given it to someone."

"Maybe you don't know you have it."

"But they know I have it and want to get it back before I find it?"

"Possibly." He pursed his lips and looked around. "And they think it's in here?"

"Apparently." He blew out a breath. "It's all just speculation, of course, but I really don't know what else to think. You and Steven worked with some of the same kids. Steven talked to Jordan and wound up dead, but you spent a lot of time with both Jordan and Steven, so maybe the people after you think one of them told you something."

"But they're not sure, so they set me up at the trailer."

"And when that fails, they keep following you and wait for a good time to strike."

"Like when we were up at the caves."

"And since they're not being very successful at killing you, they go looking for whatever it is they think you have."

"Which brings us back to this office." She looked around and shook her head. "I'm clueless." Sabrina scrubbed her rubber-encased palm down her cheek as she tried to process everything.

Clay pinched the bridge of his nose. "Do you work at home?"

"Yes. Sometimes." She pointed to the laptop on the floor. "And that's what I use. Or did use." With a gloved hand, he picked up the laptop, set it on the desk and opened it. Sabrina moved closer to him. "They weren't after that. They would have taken it."

He lifted his gaze to hers. "You're probably right."

"Do you think they were looking for something that would tell them where Jordan went?"

"It's possible."

She bit her lip. "We better check on his grand-parents."

"I'll take care of that." He got on his cell phone and called one of the other deputies on duty. After a short conversation, Clay hung up. "Leighann Sims is going to check on them."

Sabrina nodded. She knew Leighann well. "Good. Thanks." She bit her lip. "I'm worried about him."

"We'll find him." He glanced at his watch. "Why don't you pack a bag and explain what's going on to your grandmother? She can come with us and the two of you can stay at my place. I'll move back into the house, and you two can have the cottage."

Sabrina shook her head. "My grandmother will never agree."

"She will if it means keeping you safe."

Granny May put up an argument, and Sabrina had to pull out the big guns. Guilt. "I won't go without you, Granny May. I won't leave you here alone now. I thought staying away would keep the danger from you, but it's not working."

"And you think if I come with you, the danger will stop?"

"No, I honestly don't, but at least we'll be surrounded by people who will do their best to keep us safe. If we stay here, we're pretty much sitting ducks."

Granny May twisted her fingers together, her anxiety level obviously through the roof. "What about my guests? I have to be here to cook for them."

Sabrina thought fast. "It's just breakfast. We'll have it catered. Mrs. Anderson can take care of the food for tomorrow. This may not take long—I pray it doesn't—but I do think it's the wise thing to do." She gestured toward her injured arm. "Someone is serious, Granny May. I don't want to see you get hurt next."

Granny May brought her hands up to cup her cheeks before she let out a low sigh and nodded. "Well, if it'll keep you safe…"

"It's the best shot we've got." She paused and touched her arm. "No pun intended."

"But what will I do all day?"

"Act like it's a vacation. Put your feet up. Relax."

Granny May stared at her as if she'd lost her mind but said nothing more about not going. She simply shook her head. "I'll go pack and call Daisy Ann about feeding the guests in the morning."

Relieved, Sabrina hugged her grandmother. "Thank you."

After the woman disappeared to go pack, Clay

tapped his watch. "I've got to go. Lance can take you two out to the ranch."

"Where are you going?"

"Prescott's in custody. I'm going to watch the interrogation."

"What? Well, why didn't you say so? Let's go." She grabbed her purse.

"Wait a minute. There's no reason for you to go. You can just head out to the ranch, and I'll be there after I finish talking to him."

Sabrina pursed her lips and narrowed her eyes. "No way. If Stan had something to do with shooting me, I want to hear him say it." She clasped her hands in front of her. "In fact, I might just ask him myself." She knew Ned probably wouldn't let her anywhere near Stan Prescott, but that wouldn't keep her from trying. "I want to know if he knows where Jordan is."

"All right, I don't have time to argue with you. I'll call my dad on the way to the station and tell him what's going on."

"Wait a minute. If Stan Prescott's in custody, then we don't need to worry about inconveniencing you. Granny May can just stay here."

Clay hesitated. "But what if he's not the one?"

She ran a hand through her hair. "Why don't we wait and see?"

Minutes later they were in his cruiser heading for the police station. The station now occupied the renovated former train station. Six years ago the town had voted to move the police headquarters to a more centralized location. The train station had undergone a one-million-dollar face-lift thanks to fund-raisers and private donations. Now it was a tourist attraction that found its way onto the lists of a lot of people who stopped in Wrangler's Corner simply to see the place.

Clay parked, and she could feel the energy radiating from him. He was eager and ready to face the man he thought might be the one trying to kill her.

Ned met them near the interrogation room.

The two-way mirror provided privacy for Sabrina and Clay. Stan Prescott sat at the table, hands clasped in front of him, head bent. Sabrina couldn't read him. He didn't look mad, guilty—or not guilty. He looked...blank.

Ned stepped into the interrogation room and took a seat across from Prescott. "Well? You got anything to say for yourself, man?"

Stan didn't even blink, just continued his empty study of his hands. Ned sighed. "Stan, we go way back. Will you let me help you out?"

At Ned's kind words, anger blazed across Stan's face and he straightened, his fingers curling into fists. Sabrina tensed. Clay did the same. As fast as the anger burned, it fizzled out. Stan slumped and shook his head. "There's no help for me, Ned. I'm pretty much done for, I reckon."

"I'm not buying that. There's still hope. At least until they close the casket."

Sabrina itched for the man to get to the point, but she knew what Ned was doing. Being friendly to get all the information possible.

After two or three more minutes of the small talk, Ned finally asked, "Do you know Sabrina Mayfield?"

"Nope."

"Never heard of her?"

Stan sniffed and rubbed his face. "Well, sure, I've heard of her. Her granny owns that B and B on Main."

"That's right. Why'd you pull a gun on Clay and her when they were at your trailer?"

Stan snorted. "They were trespassing. I got a right to keep people off my property."

"True, true, but you didn't drop the rifle when Clay told you to."

"I was afraid of him. Thought he was going to shoot me."

"Should have," Clay muttered.

"No, you shouldn't have."

"Yeah, I know."

Ned leaned forward. "Do you know where Jordan Zellis is?"

"Who?"

Sabrina thought Prescott's confusion seemed genuine enough.

"Really?" Clay shook his head. "He's going to play that game?" He shoved his hands into his pockets. She wondered if it was because he was trying to refrain from going through the window to shake a confession out of the man.

"All right, then did you shoot at Clay and Sabrina up near the caves?"

"Shoot at them? No!"

"He does look outraged, doesn't he?" Sabrina said.

"Outraged. Yes, he does."

"He looks like he's telling the truth."

Clay raised a brow. "When you've had as much practice at lying as Stan has, you get real good at it."

Sabrina looked back at the man and felt pity for him. He looked…sad. As if he had the weight of the world on his shoulders. "I don't think he's the one who shot me."

Clay looked skeptical. "Why not?"

She shrugged and sucked in her breath as her wound pulled. "Call it a gut feeling. I don't know."

"Well, I'm not going to discount your gut, but I'm partial to evidence."

"But we don't have any against him."

Ned stood and paced from one end of the little room to the other.

"We've got his rifle," Clay said. "Ballistics is comparing it to the bullets found at the scene."

"They actually found the bullets up near the caves?"

"Yes."

"Oh. That's good."

Ned turned and walked toward the door. He tossed a glance at the two-way mirror and Clay tensed again. "Here he goes."

"What?"

"Watch."

Ned reached into his back pocket and pulled out a plastic bag with a small black item in it. He tossed it onto the table in front of Ned. "One last thing before we finish. Why was Steven Starke's wallet found in your trailer?"

Stan blinked, then stared at the sheriff. "I don't know."

Clay deflated like a punctured balloon.

"What?" Sabrina asked.

"He didn't react the way we were hoping."

"React how?"

"Like a guilty man."

TEN

Clay was not a happy man. He was afraid Sabrina's gut was right and Stan wasn't the man they were after.

But if not him, then who? "Let's go get you settled at the ranch. I want to think things through."

"What about checking the abandoned mill for Jordan and Trey?"

"I'm going to do that without you."

"What? Why?"

Her outrage didn't move him. "It's not safe, Sabrina. Someone managed to follow us up to the caves and shot you. You should be resting anyway."

"I want to go. Jordan came to me for help, and I failed him. I need to do this."

Her words bit at him. He knew how it felt to think you'd failed someone who needed you.

He sighed. "Fine. Fine. But this time you're staying in the car. With the doors locked."

"Why? Bullets can't go through windows?"

He groaned. "You're staying at the ranch."

"I'm sorry. I'm being difficult, aren't I?"

"Very."

She gave a humorless laugh. "So, we go to the mill?"

He still hesitated, and she kept her gaze steady on his. "Yes, we'll go to the mill." He looked at the sky. "It looks like snow, doesn't it?"

"Yes. I hope it holds off. I'm not in the mood to battle the weather in addition to everything else."

"I'm with you on that one," he murmured.

Her phone rang as he headed for the highway. "Hello?" She listened, and he frowned when she gasped, "Oh, no. We'll be right there."

"What is it?"

Her fingers curled around the phone. "My grandmother fell and they're taking her to the hospital."

At the next intersection, Clay whipped the car in the direction of the hospital. Her white, pinched face pulled at his heart. "What's wrong with her?"

"They think she's broken her hip."

"Oh, no. You said she fell? Where? How?"

"She was getting out of Lance's car, and she just stepped wrong and went down."

"Hang on—we'll be there soon." His phone rang and he snagged it on the second ring. "What's up, Ned?"

"Not good news, I'm afraid."

"What do you mean?" He braced himself.

"The forensics team found something up at the caves."

"Yeah?"

"They found your uncle Abe's ball cap."

"My uncle's? How do you know it's his?" Clay asked. But he knew. Everyone in Wrangler's Corner knew his uncle wore one hat. A beat-up old Yankees cap he'd gotten when he'd gone to New York six years ago to see his favorite baseball team play. "Ned, that hat could have been up there for days. Weeks, even. There's no way to know if it was left today."

"I saw him in town eating at the diner this morning. He had it on."

Clay fell silent.

"Several hairs were found in it, as well as dandruff. All it'll take is a DNA test, but I think you and I both know what's going to come back," Ned said.

"Or he can just tell you it's his and why you found it there. There's an explanation, Ned. My uncle wouldn't shoot at me."

"He's a mighty bitter man, Clay. He might very well shoot at the daughter of the woman who stood him up at the altar."

It saddened Clay to think Ned would believe that. "No, he wouldn't."

"Just wanted you to know. I'm going to pick

him up and question him. You're not welcome, you hear me?"

Clay sighed. "Yeah. I hear you." He didn't want to be there anyway. Uncle Abe would have some good reason for being up there at the caves and for losing his cap. No way would he be taking pot-shots at anyone.

Would he?

No. Of course he wouldn't. No sense wasting his time worrying about it. He kept his gaze on the rearview mirror. "I'll talk to you later, Ned."

A silver truck had been following him for the past mile or so. Normally he would probably notice but not be too worried. Unfortunately, normal had gone down the drain the minute someone started taking shots at Sabrina.

"What is it?" she asked.

"That truck behind us. Do you recognize it?"

She turned in the seat. "It's too far back."

"But it's closing in pretty fast, and we're coming up on a pretty sharp curve."

She gasped.

"What?"

"I think that's the same truck that tried to run me off the road right after Steven's funeral."

Clay gripped the wheel. "Hang on."

"What are you going to do?"

"Try and get a license plate."

* * *

Sabrina gripped the armrest and kept her eyes on the truck. The closer it got, the more certain she was that it was the same front grill she'd had riding her bumper the day of Steven's funeral. "It's him," she whispered. "Definitely."

Clay pressed the gas pedal and they shot forward. The truck closed the gap without effort.

"Clay, the curve."

"I know."

"If we go over, it'll just look like you were driving too fast." She paused and her breathing increased to keep time with her racing pulse. "Which you are."

"Just hold tight." His eyes never left the mirror. How was he staying in the lane? "All right, you ready?"

"For?"

"A little defensive driving. Here we go."

Her fingers tightened and he whipped the car into the other lane. The oncoming-traffic lane. He slammed on the brakes and the cruiser screeched a few feet before stopping. The truck sped past and braked just as hard as Clay had. Smoke from the abused tires filled the air.

And then they were moving again. Pulling up close to the truck. "Can you see it?"

She read it off to him.

The truck sat for a fraction of a second before

the driver floored the gas and roared forward. Clay got on his radio and called for backup. "Ned, I need you to run a plate for me. Nine-eight-seven-Q-L-M. I'm following the truck, headed west on Brighton Road."

The truck lurched forward, spun around the next curve and hit the exit for the highway. Sabrina bit her lip against a scream as the truck rocked, swerved and then jumped the median. "He's going the wrong way!"

Brakes squealed and tires smoked. Clay followed, siren blaring. A loud pop sounded. Then the car jerked. Clay stomped the brakes and pulled to the side of the road. He slammed a hand against the steering wheel. Sabrina gasped. *Breathe, girl, breathe.* "What just happened?"

"He got away and we've got a flat tire."

"Did he shoot it out?"

"No, just an accident."

"But you got the plate. You'll be able to find out who the truck belongs to now, right?"

"Yes indeed. Just waiting on Ned to let me know." Clay climbed from the car and opened the trunk. Within fifteen minutes, he had the flat changed and the tool tossed into the trunk.

"Come on, let's get out of here."

Sabrina shivered and gladly climbed back into the car. Clay had said it was too dangerous for her to sit in the vehicle while he changed the tire. "I don't want to take a chance on some crazy speeder losing control and running into us."

Of course, he'd been right there at the car changing the tire, so she'd appointed herself the watch person, ready to warn him if anyone got too close. No one had and soon they were on their way.

As they drove to the hospital, Sabrina's mind whirled. She desperately wanted to find Jordan, but she had to make sure her grandmother was all right. "Will someone watch over her while she's in the hospital?"

"Of course. I don't know if Ned has a deputy who can stay on her room 24/7, but we'll figure something out."

Sabrina twisted her fingers together as Clay drove. Jordan and Trey were the key. She had to find them.

As though he could read her mind, Clay said, "Okay, forget about Stan Prescott. He's probably not our guy, although I'm having trouble with the fact he had Steven's wallet in his trailer. But for now, go through everyone else who had any connection with you and Steven."

"I have, Clay, and I'm coming up with the same names. We need to find Jordan or Trey Wilde. I honestly believe they're our key to this mess."

He turned left onto the main road that would take them to the hospital. "Unfortunately, I'm in agreement. I've talked to all the other deputies and while they seemed to resent me taking over Steven's spot on the force initially, they've warmed up to me in the last couple of days."

"Why would they resent you?"

He shrugged. "Steven was their buddy. I'm an outsider."

She frowned. "You grew up in this town, the same as Steven. You're no outsider."

He shot her a smile. "I am when it comes to their close-knit group."

She harrumphed. "That's the silliest thing I've ever heard. A clique? In a police force?"

"It's okay. I get it. I didn't take it personally."

"Well, I would have."

Clay squeezed her hand and turned into the parking lot of the hospital. He took the police parking spot and threw the car in Park. They hurried into the revolving door. Sabrina rushed to the information desk and the woman seated in the chair. Sabrina had graduated high school with her. "Cyndi, I'm looking for my grandmother. Yvonne Mayfield."

"Sabrina! How are you? I heard about you getting shot. Are you all right?"

"I'm fine. Sore but fine." Cyndi's concern touched her. "The bullet only grazed me. What I really want to know is how my grandmother's doing."

Cyndi went for the keyboard. A few clicks later, she said, "She's still in the E.R."

Sabrina headed that way, throwing a "thanks" over her left shoulder.

Clay followed at her heels. "Hey, slow down."

"I can't, Clay. She wouldn't be in this situation if it weren't for me." Tears threatened, and she swallowed, refusing to let them flow. She stepped into the elevator and blinked hard. Clay stood beside her for the one-floor ride.

"It's not your fault. She stepped wrong getting out of a car. It could have happened anywhere."

"I know you're right," she whispered. "But I still feel guilty." When the doors opened, she bolted for the triage station. "I'm Yvonne Mayfield's granddaughter. May I see her?"

"Of course." The young man, who looked to be in his mid-twenties, hit a few keys on his keyboard. "She's already been taken back. Room eleven."

"Thanks."

Sabrina waited for him to press the button to unlock and open the double doors. Clay placed a hand on the small of her back to guide her down the hallway. She didn't need any help, but she took great comfort in having him there with her.

She stopped in front of the room, braced her hand on the door and took a deep breath. And then Clay was pulling her into a hug. She leaned against him, savoring his strength, trying to tug some of it into her own being. The feel of his arms around her, her nose buried against the second button of his shirt uniform helped. A lot. *You can do this. You can be strong for Granny May.*

She pulled back and smiled up at him, ignoring the fact that it felt more like a grimace. "Thanks."

"So this is what you two are up to while an old woman takes a tumble. How very respectful of you."

The grave sarcasm jolted Sabrina. She spun out of Clay's embrace to find Abe Starke staring at the two of them. His malevolent expression slapped her in the face. She took a step back and felt Clay steady her.

"Uncle Abe. What are you doing here?"

"I brought Mrs. Yvonne in. Lance got a call, and I told him I'd bring her." He sneered at Sabrina. "If this is how you show your concern, playing kissy-face outside her hospital room, I'd hate to see what you have planned when she dies."

Sabrina gaped, nausea churning in her stomach. Clay turned red. Chili pepper–red. He took a step toward his uncle and she laid a hand on his arm. "Don't," she said, her voice low. "He's not worth it."

This time Abe's face flushed. "I'll show you who's worth it, you little—"

"Enough!" Clay's roar echoed around the E.R. They had the full attention of the E.R. staff and everyone in the hallway. "Sabrina, go check on your grandmother."

She pushed open the door, stepped inside and

let the wooden door shut. She took a deep breath and closed her eyes, whispering prayers for divine intervention. "Please, Lord, take control of this crazy situation."

"Amen," came the weak voice from the bed.

Sabrina moved forward to take her grandmother's hand. "Granny May, are you all right?"

"Not so much, my dear. I fell."

"I heard." She squeezed her grandmother's fingers. "I'm so sorry."

"Trust me, I am, too, but they've given me some medication for pain and I'm feeling a bit better. I just have to be real still so it doesn't hurt so bad."

"Good. Granny May?"

"Mmm-hmm?"

"Why did Abe Starke bring you to the hospital?"

"I suppose because he felt bad he was the reason I fell."

Clay stared at his uncle and waited for the man to say something. But he just stared back, lips tight, anger burning like a hot fire in his eyes. Clay finally relaxed his stance. "I don't want to fight with you, but I won't put up with your ugly, unwarranted comments or slurs against Sabrina."

Abe acted as if he might fire back a response, but he shut his mouth, turned on his heel and walked toward the exit.

Clay followed. As soon as Abe hit the parking lot, Clay confronted him. "Why was your ball cap found up at the caves where someone shot at Sabrina and me?"

Abe froze midstep, then swiveled to face Clay. "What'd you say?"

"You heard me."

Abe's fingers curled into fists at his sides. "Yeah. I did, but I thought I must have been mistaken."

"Why were you up there?"

"Well, I wasn't shooting at you or that girl in there. I might have a lot of hate for her mama and I might not want to have her presence forced on me, but I wouldn't shoot her." Clay thought he saw a flash of hurt on the man's face before he covered it up.

"I really didn't think you would. In fact, that's what I told Ned when he asked me about it."

Abe blinked, then relaxed a fraction. "You did?"

"I did. So what were you doing up there?"

Abe sighed and shook his head. "None of your business, but I sure wasn't shooting at you."

"Come on, Abe. Ned's going to want to talk to you. They've got your hat and your DNA. They can place you in the area around the time of the shooting."

Abe ran a hand through his still-thick dark hair. "I wasn't there. I mean, I was, but I never heard any shots, so I was there either after or before."

"Doing what?"

Abe's expression darkened. "Like I said, none of your business." A muscle jumped in his jaw as he looked behind Clay in the direction of the hospital. "You stay away from her if you don't want to get your heart broken. She's trouble, just like her mama." Abe didn't wait for Clay to respond. He turned his back and left. Clay stared after the man for a brief moment, then made his way back to Sabrina. He knocked and waited for permission to enter.

When he stepped inside, he found Sabrina seated at her grandmother's side. She glanced up. "Everything all right?"

"Yes. Fine." He could see the questions in her eyes but didn't want to say anything in front of Granny May. "Or it will be." He looked at her grandmother. "Ned's going to have someone watching your room. You'll be safe here."

A knock on the door spun them all around. Clay relaxed slightly as the doctor stepped in carrying a laptop computer. "Well, Mrs. Mayfield, I hate to tell you this, but your hip is broken. You'll need surgery."

Sabrina let out a pained sigh, and Granny May groaned. "Well, I figured."

"I've already called Dr. Nathan Ray from Nashville. He's an orthopedist and one of the best in the country. You'll be in good hands."

"When will she have the surgery?" Sabrina asked.

"Within the next hour would be my guess. He was climbing in the car as we spoke." He shut the laptop. "The nurses will get you prepped, and then I'll be back to check on you when he gets here."

The nurse came in and administered more pain medication. Granny May soon drifted off, and Clay took Sabrina's hand in his. "Abe said he wasn't there at the caves when you were shot."

"Did you really expect him to admit it?"

"No, but I think I believe him."

Sabrina frowned and stood to pace to the window. "Of course you would believe him—he's your uncle."

A shot of anger splintered through him, and he closed his eyes to let it pass. "It's not that. He was doing something up there, but he wasn't shooting at us."

"What was he doing?"

"I don't know. He wouldn't tell me."

Sabrina sighed. "I guess Ned will question him."

"Yes."

"Is he going to be mad you talked to him first?" She turned to look at him, and the defeat in her eyes hurt.

He strode to her and slipped his arms around her. She didn't protest, just leaned against him. "Probably."

"What now?"

"Granny May will have her surgery, you'll move

into the cottage, and we'll keep you safe while we keep looking for Jordan and Trey."

"When will it end?" she whispered.

He placed a finger under her chin and lifted her face to his. "I can't tell you that. All I can promise is to do my best to keep you safe."

She studied him, and then her gaze dropped to his lips and a flush heated her cheeks. It wasn't a stretch to figure out what she was thinking. Which was okay because he was thinking the same thing.

Clay lowered his head and pressed a light kiss to her lips. He meant to comfort, to let her feel he was there for her. She returned the pressure, and he tightened his embrace to pull her into a bear hug. She shifted and rested her cheek against his chest and Clay decided he could stay like this just about forever.

Unfortunately, he had a potential killer to find, a possible witness to locate and two women to keep safe.

ELEVEN

No one breathed easier than Sabrina when the doctor came into the waiting room to tell her that Granny May had come through the surgery just fine but was still heavily sedated. "Go home and get some sleep. Come back tomorrow when she's awake. Otherwise you're going to be without sleep tonight and feel lousy tomorrow when she'll need you."

Clay drove her home and helped her pack a few things she might need for the next week. "I hope this doesn't drag on that long," she muttered with a frown.

"Getting tired of me already?" he teased.

"You? No. Being a target? Yes." She threw the small suitcase into the back of her car. "I'll follow you. I don't want to be without my car."

"But you won't be going anywhere without me."

She crossed her arms. "I want my car."

Clay threw his hands up. "Fine."

She gave a satisfied nod and climbed behind the

wheel. Knowing her grandmother was safe made all the difference for Sabrina as she renewed her determination to figure out why someone wanted her dead. She glanced around her neighborhood and shivered. Was the person watching her leave? Was he wondering where she was going?

Was he going to follow? She sent up a prayer asking for protection for her and those she loved. She found herself picturing Clay's face during that prayer and her next shiver had nothing to do with fear of an unknown attacker but was more of an apprehension about her growing feelings for a man whose family had no desire for them to be together.

She followed Clay for the fifteen-minute drive to his ranch. When they pulled up to the cottage, she could see the mountains in the distance, the hills with the caves and where they'd found evidence that Abe Starke had been up there. Was she crazy moving so close to a man who couldn't stand the sight of her?

She climbed out of the car and waited for Clay. "Are you sure this is a good idea? Abe hates me."

"He doesn't hate you—he hates the reminder you represent. He'll come around."

Sabrina lifted a brow and didn't comment. Voicing her doubts would gain her nothing. Time would prove who was right. She grabbed her suitcase and rolled it toward Clay's home.

Clay's home. Another set of butterflies took up residence in her belly.

He opened the door for her, and she stepped inside. It shouted "Boys only." She couldn't see a woman's touch anywhere. It was clean, just bare. Her fingers itched to do something with it.

But that wasn't her place. This was going to be her safe house. She hoped. "Thank you."

"It's small but functional. It's a two-bedroom. Kitchen to the right, hall to the left. Bedrooms on either side. Guest bedroom is on the right."

"Okay."

"I won't be far away. There's an intercom system with all the cottages on the property. You can disable it if you want or leave it on. If you need something, all you have to do is hit the button and it beeps in the main house. Mom and Dad used to rent these out before Mom got sick. Once she recovered, she was still too weak to handle being responsible for taking care of guests and Dad was working in town at the body shop and trying to keep the ranch going." He cleared his throat. "I didn't realize it until you told me about their financial issues just how much they've struggled to keep this place going." He shook his head. "I can't believe how blind I was."

"You weren't here. How were you supposed to see it?"

"I just should have."

She wouldn't argue with him. She knew how it felt to blame yourself for something you had no control over. "It's very nice. I'm sure I'll be very comfortable here." She swallowed. He dwarfed the living area. His musky scent surrounded her and she was sure he could see her pulse beating in her throat.

"All right then, I'll see you in the morning. Just call or press the button if you need anything. The fridge is full. Help yourself."

"You're leaving?"

"I'm going to help Dad with the horses. Need to bring them in from the pasture and feed them."

"Oh. Okay."

He tilted his head. "I'd invite you along, but I'd prefer you not be out in the wide-open spaces."

He was worried about a sniper. The thought chilled her. "I'll stay here. You go help your father. I'm going to call to check on Granny May and then go to bed." He stepped close and slid his arms around her. She took a deep breath and hugged him back. "Thank you, Clay," she whispered.

He kissed the top of her head. "You're welcome, Sabrina. Get some rest."

And then he was gone.

Sabrina looked around the small house. She would be fine here. She would. She really would. Wouldn't she?

* * *

Clay found his mother and the two children in the kitchen mixing a bowl of chocolate. "Brownies?"

"Yes." She looked up, flour on her cheeks and happiness in her eyes for the first time since he'd come home for Steven's funeral. "They'll be ready in about thirty minutes."

Tony, chocolate smeared all over his chin, held up the spoon. "Wanna taste?"

Clay laughed and ruffled the boy's hair. "Thanks, but I'll wait to try the finished product."

Maria smiled at him, her shy dimples putting in a rare appearance. He tapped her nose and she giggled.

Seth sat at the table, leg propped on the chair next to him, crutches on the floor. He had his laptop open. "Where's Dad? Has he left yet?"

Seth finally looked up. "Yep, he's up in the north pasture rounding up the horses."

"It's going to be a cold one tonight. Supposed to snow, too," his mother said.

Great. He liked the snow, just not when he was trying to keep a killer from succeeding in getting his latest target. The thought of being trapped in one place made that spot between his shoulders itch. He tugged his hat down around his ears. "I thought he was going to wait on me."

"I did, too, but you know your father."

"What about the barbecue? Are you going to cancel?"

Her eyes sharpened. "Not a chance."

"But—"

"But nothing. We'll move it into the barn and the house if we need to."

"If you say so."

"I say so." His mother turned her attention back to the children and the brownies. Seth's frown deepened as he focused on the computer.

"What's wrong?" Clay asked him.

His brother slammed the laptop shut. "Looks like someone I know is in trouble."

"What kind of trouble?"

"I don't know. Nothing I can do about it anyway."

"Right." Clay blew out a breath and headed for the barn. As he pulled on his gloves, he noticed the light on in the kitchen of the cottage where he'd tucked Sabrina. He hoped she was able to rest tonight.

Darkness was falling fast. He hopped into one of the golf carts his father kept to navigate the acres and aimed it for the north pasture.

Whistles and yells clued him in to his father's location. The horses headed his way. Clay turned the cart to get behind them.

"'Bout time you showed up!" his dad yelled as he thundered past him on a large black stallion.

"Sorry! I'll get the stragglers."

Clay stomped the gas pedal, and the cart bolted forward. The horses ran from him toward the barn. Once they realized they were heading in, it didn't take much to convince them to move that way.

He slowed to watch the sunset. The ranch really was a beautiful place, but he just had no interest in running it. He was a cop. First and foremost. Dealing with his sister's bullies—albeit the wrong way initially—and landing himself in trouble had been wrong, but it had also led Ned to take him under his wing and teach him how to fight injustice.

With a badge.

And now injustice looked as if it was getting the upper hand.

His phone rang. Ned. "What's up?"

"I can't find your uncle. You have any idea where he is?"

"Where've you looked?"

"I'm at his house right now. No sign of him."

Clay sighed. "He was at the hospital earlier, but I don't know where he went after he left there. If I see him, I'll give you a call."

"Thanks. I need to hear from him why his hat was up at the caves."

"I know. He'll have a good reason." He just didn't know if the man would share it.

He sniffed. Straightened.

Smoke? "Where's that coming from?"

"What?"

"Nothing. I've gotta go. If I see Abe again, I'll call you."

Clay ended the call and started moving, trying to determine the direction of the smoke. As he drove toward the grove of trees near the pond, the smell grew stronger.

And stronger.

His heart thudded. If there was a fire, they were in trouble.

But he didn't see flames. He got to the edge of the trees and stopped, unholstered his weapon and headed in the direction he thought the smoke came from.

Just inside the copse of trees, he stopped. Someone had placed a ring of rocks on the ground. In the midst of them, a small fire burned. "Hey! Who's out here?"

Her heart pounded in her ears. Her lungs felt full of fluid. Sabrina woke with a gasp, her fingers clutching the covers, her ears straining to hear every little sound in the unfamiliar house.

Memory returned. She was in Clay's guest room. She relaxed a fraction until she heard the footstep in the hall.

Terror froze her for a split second. Then she tucked her injured arm against her and rolled from the bed onto the floor. The cold hardwood chilled her already shivering body. Should she call out? Or just wait?

Another footfall just outside her door.

Sabrina trembled. Her phone. Where had she put it?

She'd left it charging on the end table. The one on the opposite side of the bed she'd just slid from.

She moved to the foot of the bed, slithering on the floor like a snake, using her one good arm, doing her best to stay silent. She peered toward the door she'd left open.

Two feet, booted toes faced her.

She bit her lip hard enough to make her flinch. Would he come in? Start looking for her? Did he know she was there or was he looking for Clay?

The feet turned, and she puffed out a relieved breath. The slow, almost silent footsteps carried her intruder away from the room into Clay's bedroom across the hall. Making as little noise as possible, Sabrina scrambled from the floor and darted around the bed to grab her phone from the nightstand. She started to bolt for the front door but froze when the footsteps headed back toward her.

She did a one-eighty and headed on bare feet to the bathroom off the guest room. With shaking fingers, she turned the lock, then pressed the button on the phone to bring up the screen. She squinted in the sudden brightness and did her best to ignore her pounding pulse and strangled breathing.

Clay or 911? Clay was closer. She dialed his number and held her breath.

Clay's phone rang as he assessed the area. Night had fallen. The darkness pressed in, broken only by the dying flames of the small campfire. He kicked dirt over it and looked at his screen. Sabrina. He smiled and answered. "Did you get a good nap?"

"Someone's in the house, Clay," she whispered.

Fear shooting through his veins, Clay bolted for the golf cart. "What do you mean? Where are you?"

"Hiding in the bathroom. I woke up when I heard footsteps in the hall. Hurry!"

"Stay on the line with me. I'm only a couple of minutes away. Do you know where he is now?"

"No. I can't hear anything." A thud sounded.

"Sabrina?"

"He's in the room, just outside the door. He's not making any effort to be quiet."

He had to strain to hear her. Her terror reached through the line and grabbed him by the throat. "I'm thirty seconds away."

Each second seemed like a lifetime until finally, the cottage came into view.

Dread pounded through him. Abe's truck sat in his parents' drive. He'd deal with him later. Clay hopped from the cart. He shoved aside his heavy coat and gripped his Glock, pulling it from the shoulder holster and holding it ready.

He stepped up onto the porch, stood to the side and twisted the knob to the front door. Unlocked. He pushed it open. When no bullets started flying, he slid inside and shut the door behind him with a faint click.

Silence greeted him. Fear clutched him. Was he too late?

Clay held the weapon gripped in front of him, pointed to the ceiling. He took gentle steps toward the bedrooms.

Then he heard the footsteps coming toward him.

Clay backed up and slid around the side of the entertainment center and waited.

When the intruder took two steps past him, Clay placed the weapon just under the man's ear. "Move and you die."

TWELVE

Sabrina heard Clay on the other end of the phone. He hadn't hung up but the sounds were muffled, making her think he'd put the phone in a pocket. She heard words. Was he talking to someone? She eased up from the bathroom floor and unlocked the door.

Cautious, tense and ready to react to any perceived threat, she stepped out into the bedroom. When nothing happened, she crept over to the door that led out into the hall.

"Are you crazy?" Clay's shout echoed through the house.

Sabrina froze. Should she go out or stay put?

Now that Clay was in the house, her fear ebbed. No bullets had been fired; no one had been hurt. At least she didn't think so. She moved toward the living area and peered around the edge of the wall.

It was still dark, but she could make out Clay's form and another man's. "Sabrina? You can come out now." Still she hesitated. "Sabrina?" Someone turned a light on. At the concern in his voice, she moved into the den.

And found herself face-to-face with Abe Starke.

"You?" she whispered.

He held up a hand. "I didn't know you were here. I was just looking for my rifle. I went up to the big house and Seth said you were out with the horses. I decided to come over here and get my gun. I didn't know she was here. I didn't."

Sabrina wilted against the wall. Relieved and furious.

Tears welled and she blinked to keep them from falling. "It's okay," she said. "You didn't know."

"I didn't. I really didn't." His face darkened and he turned to Clay. "What's she doing here?"

"I'm trying to keep her safe. Obviously I'm doing a lousy job of it." He ran a hand through his hair, not hiding his agitation.

"What's going on in here?"

Sabrina jerked toward the door. Abe and Clay spun, too. Clay's father stood there, rifle in hand, eyes narrowed. "Abe?"

Abe threw his hands up as Clay glared. "Your gun is safe where it is. I'll call Ned. I'm sure he wants to question you in the shooting."

Clay's father narrowed his eyes. "I'll take him in. I want to talk to him anyway."

"I don't think that's a good idea." Clay pulled his phone from his pocket and dialed Ned's number. He filled the sheriff in, and Ned promised to head over.

Abe snorted. "That woman got you hog-tied already, don't she, boy?"

Clay shook his head, and Sabrina watched his neck turn red. She admired his restraint. Personally, she wanted to smack his uncle. Not that it would help the situation. Other than making her feel better. "I'll leave."

"You won't," Clay said.

"She better," Abe snarled. He looked at his brother. "If she's not gone by morning, you can forget saving the ranch. Better start selling stuff off, because you won't get a penny of my money."

Ross turned white, and Clay flinched. "What are you talking about, Abe?"

"Nothing," his father nearly shouted. He took a deep breath. "Nothing." He gripped his brother's arm and shot a look back at Clay. "We'll be outside talking while we wait on Ned."

"No. We won't. There won't be any talking until she's gone."

Ross studied his brother, looked at Clay, then Sabrina. Then back to Abe. "Then I guess we don't have anything left to talk about. Once you're gone, don't bother coming back."

Abe blinked, then frowned. "You sure you want to do that?"

Ross pinched the bridge of his nose, then met

his brother's gaze. "No. I don't. But I'll do what's right. All my life I've taught my kids to do the right thing. Do you know how many times I preached that even when faced with hardship, you still do the right thing?" He straightened his shoulders. "So I'm going to practice what I preach. You're my brother, and I love you. But you get off my land and don't come back until you've gotten rid of that chip of bitterness you got riding your shoulders."

Abe looked as though he might self-combust. Sabrina held her breath and looked from one man to the next. Had Clay's father really just done what she thought he'd done?

Without another word, Abe left the cottage.

"Dad—"

Ross held up a hand. "Not now, son. We'll talk later. Take care of your lady and I'll see you in the morning." And then he was gone, following Abe onto the front porch.

Clay stared after his father. Sabrina slipped back into the bedroom and started throwing her things into the small suitcase.

"What are you doing?"

She didn't turn, just continued packing. "I'm leaving. I won't be the cause of trouble with your family."

Clay sighed. "It's not you. I'm not sure, but I think that was a long time in coming."

She stilled. "What do you mean?"

He glanced out the window. "Nothing. Ned's here. Let me go take care of Abe. I'll be back. Please don't leave yet."

Sabrina warred with the desire to just run away and the need to hear him out. He won. She left her bag on the bed and let him take her hand and lead her to the couch in his den. He picked up the remote on the coffee table, aimed it at the fireplace and powered up the gas logs.

She stared at the flames, silently wishing she could aim a remote at her troubles and let them go up in smoke. She could hear the four men talking on the porch even though Clay had shut the door behind him. Abe's defiance carried. Finally, Clay stepped back inside, a frown on his face.

"What's going to happen now?" she asked.

"Ned will talk to Abe and fill me in tomorrow."

She nodded. "Your parents are having a tough time. From what Abe said, it sounds like he's helping your parents out financially. If he cuts that off, they could lose the ranch. I won't let that happen when all I have to do is leave."

"Well, you can't leave tonight. Get some sleep. I don't have an alarm system on this house, but Seth and I can take turns keeping watch. I don't think he's sleeping much these days anyway. Watching this place might be a good distraction for him."

"How did he break his leg?"

"He got distracted."

"Seth? Distracted?" She gave a short laugh of disbelief. "He's the most focused person I know. Seth doesn't get distracted."

Clay reached out and ran a hand down the side of her cheek. "I can think of only one thing that might have distracted him."

Sabrina shivered at his gentle touch. "What?"

He smiled. "A woman."

"Oh."

"Yeah. You've certainly distracted me."

"I have?"

"Uh-huh." He moved closer, homing in on her lips. "Have I distracted you?"

She knew if he looked, he'd see her pulse pounding in her throat. "A bit. Maybe."

"Maybe?"

She reached up and cupped his chin. "You distract me from my fear. When you're with me, I'm not so scared."

Tenderness gazed back at her. He pressed a light kiss to her lips and pulled her into a hug. "I'm glad," he whispered against her ear. "And now I'm going to go."

"Okay." She clung to him a moment longer, then backed away. "Thank you."

"Get some rest." His jaw hardened. "I promise no one will bother you again tonight. And tomorrow we're going to find Jordan or Trey. Or both."

"I sure hope so. I don't know how much more of this I can handle."

He paused at the door, hand on the knob. "You know, after all that happened with Steven, I kind of pushed God away. I figured He'd let me down when He let Steven get killed. Like He just didn't care anymore or something."

"It's understandable."

"Understandable maybe, but it doesn't make it right. At the time I should have been leaning on my faith more than ever, I discounted it, treated it like it wasn't important or wasn't real." He let go of the doorknob and studied her. "And then He brings me home and drops you into my life."

She bit her lip and lowered her eyes. "I know. I've been nothing but trouble, and I'm sorry."

He moved fast. He gripped her hands and pressed his forehead to hers. "No. I was going to say God must still care." He kissed her again, soft and sweet and lingering. "He knew I needed you and I'm thankful that He's showing me He really does care."

Wow. Sabrina had no words.

"'Night, Sabrina."

"Good night, Clay," she whispered.

She watched him walk away and disappear into his parents' house. Then she touched her lips and gave a small smile. Which promptly melted into a frown. "God, I know You care. You're letting some wonderful things happen in spite of the bad. But could You please help us find something that would lead us to the person trying to kill me?" She locked the dead bolt and walked back into Clay's guest bedroom. "I really don't want to die yet. I have too much to live for."

THIRTEEN

Clay hadn't slept much last night, but thankfully, he wasn't feeling the effects of the restless night. He'd spent much of the wee hours watching the cottage, even going so far as to walk the perimeter several times.

Seth had been more than happy to take watchdog duty, had even opened up a little to Clay and admitted he was pining over a woman he'd left behind on the rodeo circuit.

He'd even explained in detail how he'd gotten hurt. He'd just settled himself on Black Death, a bull almost no one could stay on for more than three seconds, when he'd looked up to find her watching. "I was glad she was there, but then Garrett Jackson walked up and put his arm around her and I saw red." He smirked. "And then I was eating dirt and screaming through a haze of pain."

"Can you do both at the same time?" Clay asked.

Seth snorted. "I managed. Then I passed out.

When I woke up, I'd been in surgery and was in the recovery room."

"And you never called Mom or Dad."

"Naw. Didn't want to worry them."

But they were worried. Every time they looked at Seth, Clay could see the worry there. At least he knew his instincts were still sharp.

"But you came home to heal."

"Yeah."

"What's her name?"

Another snort and a black look. "Trouble." And that was all Seth had had to say.

This morning Clay found his brother sitting at the table, casted leg propped up on the chair beside him, newspaper open. A platter of scrambled eggs, bacon and toast sat on the table. He looked up when Clay entered. "You get any sleep?"

"A couple hours," Clay said. "You?"

"'Bout the same."

"Where are Mom and the kids?"

"She took Tony to school. Maria rode with her." He munched a piece of bacon, then said, "Phone rang this morning."

"I heard it." Clay went straight for the coffee-pot and dumped what had been brewed two hours ago. He fixed a fresh batch—double strength—and stood in front of it with his mug in hand.

"It was Ned. Said to let you sleep if you were

sleeping, but when you woke up, to tell you they found Trey Wilde."

Clay whirled. "Why didn't you wake me?"

Seth lifted a brow. "Because Ned said not to."

"Since when do you do everything you're told?" Clay grabbed his cell phone, filled his mug with the brewed coffee and took a seat at the table.

Ned answered before the first ring finished. "Figured you'd be calling."

"You have Trey?"

"Unfortunately, the coroner has him in Nashville."

Clay slumped, coffee forgotten, grief for the waste of a young life consuming him. "Ah, man..."

Seth looked up with a frown and a question in his eyes. Clay ignored him for now.

"Knew that boy since he was just an infant." Ned's voice thickened and he cleared his throat. "He was in trouble all the time, but—"

"Yeah."

"Yeah."

A pause. "So how'd he die?" Clay asked.

This time Seth put his coffee on the table and leaned forward as though he wanted to hear the conversation.

"Bullet to the back of the head," Ned said.

Clay winced. "These people aren't playing around, Ned."

"No, they're not. The medical examiner has

him now. He's being held as a John Doe. Coroner said he was found three days ago. When we put the BOLO out on Trey and Jordan, the coroner saw the news and recognized him. Thanks to the cold temps, he's still in pretty good shape. But get this—you know that license plate you gave me to run?"

"Yes."

"I got so busy I forgot to tell you. It's registered to Travis Wilde."

"Trey's father."

"You get the gold star."

Clay sighed and pressed his fingers against his eyes as he thought. "All right, so they killed Trey. Did he have anything on him that might tell us who his killer is?"

"Nothing. Not a thing. No ID, nothing. The ME's doing the autopsy. Hopefully, she'll have something for us soon."

"Have you notified Trey's parents?"

"Yes. They're devastated."

He could only imagine. He thought about his parents' grief and then his own with losing Steven. Having a sibling die was bad. Very, very bad. Losing a child? He couldn't fathom it. "I'm worried about Jordan, Ned."

"I am, too. Which is why I've got everyone looking for him right now." He blew out a sigh. "How is Sabrina?"

"She's safe for now." He got up and looked out the window at his little cottage on the small hill. "But I have to say, I'm more scared than ever for her at this point."

"I can't say I blame you. Just keep an eye on her. Don't let her go anywhere alone."

"I won't, but you know we've got the Christmas barbecue coming up on Saturday."

"Would your parents consider canceling it?"

"What do you think?"

"Right. Then she'll just have to stay out of sight."

Clay rubbed his chin and realized Seth still hadn't taken his eyes off him. He was going to have to fill his brother in on a few more details when he hung up.

The light in the cottage kitchen went on, and he figured Sabrina was up and fixing coffee. She'd want to go to the hospital to check on her grandmother.

"What did you do with Prescott?"

"Convinced him to check into a rehab facility in Nashville."

"Voluntarily?"

"It was either that or jail."

"Ah." Ned. The man who always believed in second chances. Clay wasn't so sure that had been a good idea. "He had Steven's wallet, Ned."

Seth's good foot hit the floor. "What?"

Clay held up a finger.

"Yeah, he had it, but there weren't any of his fingerprints on it."

"So he wiped it clean." Clay volunteered the words, but his heart wasn't in them. He didn't believe Stan had anything to do with Steven's death. Not really. But if not him, then who?

Whoever killed Trey and whoever had Jordan on the run, that's who. "Has Lance uncovered anything on where Jordan might be?"

"No. Trey's body was found not too far from the abandoned mill. I've got Lance staking the place out today. If Jordan's there, we'll nab him."

"Right. In the meantime, I've got a lady to protect."

"How are the kids?"

"They ask about Jordan every day but seem to be pretty happy here."

"Good."

"What did Abe have to say about his whereabouts when Sabrina was catching a bullet?"

"A lot. And…I don't think he was shooting at you or Sabrina."

Clay frowned. "What makes you say that?"

"He took me up to the caves. There's a tree up there with his initials carved in it—his and Sabrina's mother's. Apparently, he goes up there all the time and talks to her."

"That's…sad."

"Yeah. Plus he let me examine all of his weapons. None matched the bullet the crime scene unit found. My other line's ringing. We'll catch up later." Ned hung up.

"Tell me what's going on. Who had Steven's wallet?" Seth demanded.

Clay took the next ten minutes to drink his coffee and fix Sabrina a plate for breakfast while he filled his brother in. His father walked into the kitchen, and Clay snapped his mouth shut. He picked up his coffee cup and drank the last drop. Seth buried his nose in the paper.

"Everything all right in here?" his father asked as he helped himself to the coffee.

"Just fine, Dad." He looked out the window. Sabrina stood on the front porch. Clay grabbed a piece of toast and Sabrina's plate and headed out the door.

Sabrina paused on the porch and waited for Clay to walk over to her. He wore a frown, and his jaw looked tight. Had he had an argument with someone?

She had her purse slung over her shoulder and her phone in her back pocket. As she watched Clay approach, she swallowed hard. He was definitely a very good-looking man. He was rough around the edges but had a gentle heart. Old-fashioned but confident enough to let his woman be herself. Just the kind of man she wanted. Needed.

His woman.

What would it be like to be his? Just the thought sent blood rushing into her cheeks.

"You feeling all right? You look a little flushed."

Sabrina cleared her throat. "I'm fine."

"You should have waited for me to come get you." He looked around. "I don't like you being out in the open like this."

Sabrina returned his frown. "I can't hibernate, Clay. I need to get to the hospital to see my grandmother."

He gestured with the plate. "I brought you some breakfast. You hungry?"

"Starving. I was going to ask if we could go through a drive-through, but this'll work." She opened the door and stepped back inside. Clay followed, his eyes on the area behind them.

They settled themselves at the kitchen table, and Sabrina helped herself to the plate of food. "Have you talked to your dad about your uncle and the ranch yet?"

"Nope. Not yet. Nothing to talk about, really. We'll figure something out." He swiped his hand across the table, his brow furrowed.

"If I leave, it would make things easier, wouldn't it?"

He looked up. "Easier? Maybe. But us Starkes have never been known for taking the easy route, so let me worry about it, all right?"

"You know that's not my personality, don't you?"

He eyed her. "Yes. I know." He cleared his throat. "I'm going to take you to see your grandmother, if that's all right. I really don't want you driving by yourself. I just don't think it's safe."

She toyed with the fork. "Ned's giving you an awful lot of leeway when it comes to protecting me. Don't you have a shift you need to be working with the department?"

He shrugged. "Ned likes you."

She smiled. "I like Ned, but you're getting paid to do a job. Protecting me 24/7 isn't exactly what the county is paying you for."

"Of course it is. You're a tax-paying citizen, too."

"Well, that's true enough, I suppose, but you know what I mean."

"I do. And in all seriousness, I'm basically doing the job as a favor to Ned. And I've already told him I was going to keep you safe. He agreed." He carried her empty plate to the sink. "What about your job? Have you talked to your boss?"

"Yes. Thankfully, she's being understanding about it. I have several days of vacation I can take if I need to. Right now I'm looking for Jordan, and that's working. Sort of."

"Good. I'd hate for either of us to lose a job over this." He picked up the coat he'd shed when they'd walked in. "You ready?"

"Yes."

"Then let's go." He placed a hand on her back and walked with her to his cruiser. The frown stayed on his face. Tension rolled from him.

"Is something else wrong? You've been distracted and tense since you walked over here."

He opened the door, and she slid into the passenger seat. Clay buckled himself into the driver's seat before he answered. "I got a call from Ned. They found Trey Wilde, and he's been killed."

She gasped. Sorrow hit her, and her throat tightened. She fought the tears clouding her eyes. "Oh, no. His poor parents. Why?"

"We don't know yet for sure, of course, but it's obvious someone thinks he knew something. On top of that, the truck that tried to run us off the road is registered to Trey's father."

"So whoever killed him stole his truck?"

"That's what it looks like."

Sabrina closed her eyes and said a prayer for Jordan. Clay drove to the hospital, and she kept an eye on the rearview mirror.

When they reached the hospital without incident, Sabrina pulled in a relieved breath. She made her way to her grandmother's room, where she found the doctor just coming out. "How is she?"

"Still sleeping. We're taking good care of her, but it's going to be a long road to recovery."

Sabrina nodded. Already her mind clicked with everything she needed to start doing.

Call her boss and ask for a leave of absence.

Check on the boarders at the B and B.

Call Daisy Ann to see if she could continue to provide the meals and be available should one of the boarders need something.

What was she forgetting?

A hand fell on her shoulder. "Lance can watch over you two while I go check in at the station."

"Thank you, Clay. For everything."

"Sure thing." He smiled.

Lance arrived fifteen minutes later, and Sabrina settled herself in to wait for her grandmother to wake up.

FOURTEEN

Saturday morning, Lance stepped into the hospital room, and Sabrina looked up from the laptop Clay had brought to her first thing Thursday morning. She'd been able to get some work done when she realized her grandmother wasn't going anywhere until the doctors discovered the reason for her fever. Between the stack of books on the end table, the computer and helping with her grandmother, she'd not had a boring moment.

"How's she doing?" Lance asked.

"Better, I think. She hasn't had a fever since yesterday afternoon, so I think we may be out of here soon. They were talking about getting her to the National Healthcare facility first thing tomorrow morning."

"Excellent."

Sabrina gave a wry smile. "I almost hate to leave. It's been so quiet. No one trying to kill me, no one breaking in during the night…nothing." She shrugged. "It's been nice."

"It's because no one wants to mess with the guard at the door."

Sabrina laughed. Lance, Clay and Leighann had all taken turns to ensure her and her grandmother's safety. "I'm very thankful to you all."

"Leighann and I are going to share the shift tonight so Clay can be at the barbecue. Aaron and Amber are coming home for it."

Clay's other brother and his sister. "Good. I think his mother needs them to be here." She glanced at the window. "What will they do if it starts to snow?"

He shrugged. "Move it indoors, I suppose."

"That's a lot of people."

"We'll work around it. It wouldn't be the first time we've done it in the snow." He gave her a gentle smile. "Don't worry. If it looks like it's going to get bad, people will stay home."

A knock on the door swung her attention from Lance to Clay as he stepped inside. "You ready?"

"Yes." She patted her grandmother's hand. "We had a good visit before the pain meds knocked her out."

Clay took her hand. "Thanks for doing this, Lance. I appreciate it."

"I'll let Leighann enjoy hanging out with you all for a while. Then I'll head over when she gets here."

"Is Krissy coming?" Clay asked.

"Yes. Her brother is with her mom so she can come."

"See you in a little while."

"Save me some barbecue."

Clay and Sabrina left the hospital. Sabrina settled into the passenger seat. "Do you think this is a good idea?"

"What?"

"Me coming to the barbecue."

"I think it's a fabulous idea." He gave a short laugh. "In fact, I think you'll be safer there than anywhere else in town. Every cop in Wrangler's Corner will be there. On duty and off. The ones on duty will come in shifts."

Sabrina nodded. "True. Okay. I'm looking forward to meeting Aaron and Amber."

"They came in last night."

She hesitated. "Is Abe going to be there?"

"I doubt it. He and my father haven't spoken since Dad told him to leave."

Sabrina dropped her head. "I'm sorry."

"It's not your fault."

And then he was pulling into the drive, and Sabrina's eyes widened at the transformation. "Wow."

Tables lined the front yard, and two large grills smoked delicious scents. Christmas lights and Christmas trees sparkled in multicolored profusion. Clay parked under a tree at the edge of the property. Sabrina climbed out and shivered. "It's cold, but the sun feels good."

"Still looks like it's going to snow, but for now it's a great day for a barbecue." Sadness flickered in his eyes for a brief moment. Then he gave a strained smile. "Steven would love it." He took her hand and led her to the house.

In the kitchen Clay introduced her to his brother Aaron. Sabrina gulped. He could be Steven's twin. "Nice to meet you."

"And you."

"Aaron's graduating from veterinarian school in about a week."

"Congratulations."

"Thanks."

Next Clay turned to a beautiful dark-haired young woman with the Starke blue eyes. "This is Amber, my wayward sister."

Amber gave her brother a light punch in the arm. "I'm not wayward—I just don't get home very often." She gave Sabrina a hug. "Glad to meet you."

"She's a writer for a travel magazine. Has the glamorous life and gets to travel all over the place looking for the next best vacation spot. At least that's what she's doing this month."

"Right. Glamorous." Amber wrinkled her nose and rolled her eyes. Sabrina loved the camaraderie between the siblings and felt a pang of loneliness.

She'd always wanted a brother or a sister. Mostly a sister. Or a big brother to beat up the bullies. Either way, she felt as if she'd missed out.

Clay's mother bustled into the kitchen followed by Tony and Maria. Sabrina hugged each child and listened to their excited chatter about living on the ranch. Amber moved to help her mother, and Aaron pushed open the storm door. "I'm going to check the grills."

Clay tapped her arm. "Can you give me a bit? I want to help my dad with the horses."

Sabrina smiled. "Sure, I'm fine. Take your time."

"Good. Thanks." He placed a kiss on her cheek. "Stay inside and hibernate. Okay?"

"The kids want to show me the barn."

He frowned, then looked outside. "That's fine, I suppose. We're going to turn a few of the horses out and muck a couple of stalls." His frown faded. "Wanna help?"

Sabrina laughed. "Sure, let me just put my purse up." Clay and the children waited for her. Then they all walked to the barn together. Once inside, she gave a start of surprise. "It's warm in here. I mean, it's not toasty like inside your cottage, but it's not cold, either."

Clay smiled. "When it gets below freezing, Dad uses the heat. He turned it on last night. Don't want the horses getting cold."

"They're spoiled animals."

"We've got some high-dollar boarders." He shrugged. "The temperature-controlled barn is one of the perks. Can't be too warm though, or the horses' body temperatures can't adjust to being in the cold."

She reached for the pitchfork, and he stopped her. "I was just kidding about helping. Your arm's still healing."

She moved it. "It's sore, but I can deal with it."

For the next thirty minutes, Clay and his father turned horses out. The children got bored with the mucking and decided to head inside for some cookies. Sabrina wasn't ready to leave, so she started forking fresh hay back in for when the horses returned. She had to admit, the arm hurt. A lot. But the exercise felt good.

Sabrina jabbed the pitchfork into the next bale of hay and winced. A slight shuffle in the loft above caught her attention.

A barn cat?

Hay rained down on her. She jumped out of the way. Something landed beside her with a thud.

She stared. A pitchfork stuck up out of the dirt. Right where she'd been standing only a second before.

"Sabrina?" She spun to see Clay standing in the door.

She pointed to the pitchfork with a shaky finger. "That just fell from the loft."

Clay strode over and looked up. He slapped a hand against the wall of the barn. "That didn't just fall." He bolted out of the barn and Sabrina followed him. They stopped and stared at the growing crowd. "It could be anyone," he muttered. "No one looks out of place."

"You know everyone here?"

"Yes."

She swallowed. "Then if the pitchfork didn't fall by itself, someone threw it at me."

"I thought you would be safe here."

Sabrina's knees refused to hold her. She grabbed his arm so she wouldn't fall over. "I don't think I'm going to be safe anywhere until this person is caught."

Clay had to agree. She wasn't safe until the person was caught. And that person was someone he knew. Someone who blended in with his family.

Someone he trusted.

A cold ball formed in his belly. Which meant now he trusted no one.

To his right he saw Ned and motioned him over.

"Great tribute to Steven," Ned said.

"Yes, it is. Unfortunately, someone just tried to kill Sabrina again."

Ned jerked and frowned. "What?"

Clay told him what had happened in the barn. "It's someone we know, Ned. It's someone here."

"Who?"

He shot him an exasperated look. "If I knew that, I would have arrested him by now."

Lance Goode drove up and his wife, Krissy, walked over to greet him. "Their body language say anything to you, Ned?"

Ned shook his head. "They're having issues."

"I kind of got that feeling, but I just thought it was from all the stress Krissy's under with her mother."

"That and she's just not happy."

"Shame."

"Yeah. I gave Lance the name of a good counselor. I hope they'll use it."

"How's Prescott doing?"

Ned blew out a sigh and held up his phone. "That's one of the reasons I wanted to get you alone. Prescott escaped."

"You're kidding me."

"I wish." Ned massaged his temple. "I made a bad call on him. I hate that."

Clay ran a hand through his hair and blew out a sigh. "All right, then. Look around and see if you spot him. It might have been him who tossed that pitchfork at Sabrina."

They split up. Clay headed straight for Sabrina. She didn't want to hibernate, but with a killer in his backyard, she might not have a choice.

FIFTEEN

Sabrina let Clay usher her into the house. Amber was playing checkers with the children, but otherwise the home was empty. "Stay in the house, okay?" Clay said. "If the person who's trying to kill you is around here somewhere, I don't want to give him another chance to get at you. Ned's going to keep an eye on one side of the house, and Lance will watch the other."

Sabrina sighed and sank into one of the kitchen chairs with a slow nod. "You're right. The children were in the barn with me for a little while. If that person had thrown the pitchfork with them in there..." She shook her head. "Fine. I agree. I don't want to put anyone else in danger. I'll stay inside."

"And I'm going to start snooping around and asking questions."

"Oh, Clay, I'm sorry. This is supposed to be a time for you to enjoy your family."

"I can't enjoy it while we've still got a missing kid and Steven's killer is running free. Sit tight.

I'm going to look for whoever could have possibly tossed that pitchfork at you. I'll be back."

He went out the door, and Sabrina looked around. The least she could do was help clean up. She rose and went to the sink, filling it with sudsy hot water to hand-wash the larger pots and pans. The smaller items went into the dishwasher.

As she scrubbed, her brain spun. What could she have that these people knew about but she didn't?

The very idea was crazy.

Amber and the children tired of their checkers and headed back outside to enjoy the barbecue while the snow was holding off, leaving Sabrina to finish cleaning. Soon she had the area spotless.

The door opened, and Clay's mother stepped inside. She blinked. "Did the cleaning fairies come?"

Sabrina laughed and raised her hand. "Just one."

The woman engulfed her in a tight hug. "I want to adopt you." Sabrina hugged her back. Mrs. Starke shook her head. "Christmas came early."

"I'm afraid there will be plenty to do when the party ends."

"Oh, yes, true enough, but at least I don't have to worry about this." She shook her head. "I think we're going to have to end it early. The sun's disappeared, and I think the snow is getting ready to fall." Her gaze landed on the family picture she had taped to the refrigerator. Her eyes teared up. "Steven should have been here."

"I know," Sabrina whispered.

"I miss him something awful."

She rubbed the grieving mother's shoulder. "I'm sure you do. Everyone who knew him loved him."

Mrs. Starke looked at her. "He talked about you, you know."

"He did?" That surprised her.

She nodded. "He said if he wasn't still grieving his wife, he might be interested in pursuing something more than a friendship with you. He said you were special."

Sabrina gave her a sad smile. "What an honor."

"I see what he meant now." She patted Sabrina's cheek, then swiped her eyes. "I need a moment."

"Of course."

The woman disappeared down the hall.

The door opened again and Krissy Goode entered. "Oh. I didn't realize anyone was in here. Lance said I could come in and get warm."

"It's just me and Mrs. Starke."

"I'll come back later."

"Did you need something?"

"No. Just wanted to get warm."

Sabrina smiled. "Have a seat."

Krissy hesitated, then lowered herself into the nearest chair. Sabrina sat opposite her. If she couldn't be outside, she could at least visit with those who came in. "It is a bit chilly, isn't it?"

"It's not too bad as long as you have a place to

warm up. The bonfire's doing a pretty good job, but those clouds look like they're getting ready to drop a few inches of snow at any moment." She twisted her fingers together and jiggled her leg. Her gaze flitted from the corner of the kitchen to the door, then back to the table.

"Is everything all right?" Sabrina asked.

Krissy smiled. A tight thin one that looked forced. "Of course. What could possibly be wrong?"

"You seem a little stressed."

"No more than usual." Her shoulders drooped. "It's just my life right now. My mom has Alzheimer's, you know."

"I know. Clay told me."

Krissy shrugged. "And I hate living in this dead-end town, but I'm stuck because Lance has no ambition. He just wants to be a small-town cop for the rest of his life, and what I want doesn't matter."

Sabrina flinched at the anger emanating from the woman. "I'm so sorry."

The anger faded and Krissy straightened. "No, I'm sorry for dumping on you."

The door opened and Clay stepped inside. When he saw them, he nodded. "Hi, Krissy."

"Hi, Clay."

Clay's gaze shot to Sabrina's. "You all right?"

"I'm fine. Staying inside like a good girl."

Krissy yawned and stood. "Guess I'll go back

outside and join Lance." She paused at the door. "Since when did you invite Stan Prescott to this thing?"

Clay went still. Sabrina froze. "What? You saw him? Here?"

"Where?" Clay demanded at the same time.

Krissy's eyes widened. "Uh…not too long ago. Out near the barn and then by the trees on the other side of the pond."

"You're sure it was him?"

Krissy rolled her eyes. "How long have I known Stan? Of course I'm sure."

And then she was gone, pushing past Clay and out through the back door.

Clay slapped the door frame. "Sit tight. I'm going to get a search party together, and we're going to find this guy. Don't worry—I'll have Lance watch the house just in case Stan decides he wants to sneak back over this way."

Then he, too, was gone.

Sabrina sat still for a minute, her mind processing the conversation with Krissy and the fact that she'd spotted Stan Prescott nearby.

She registered a noise coming from the hallway. She rose and followed the sound until she stood just outside the doorway of the master bedroom.

She hesitated, then peeked around the corner. And her heart broke.

Mrs. Starke sat on the king-size bed, hugging a

picture frame to her chest. Sabrina had no doubt it was a picture of Steven.

She started to turn to leave the mother alone with her grief when a box caught her eye. Other items rested on the comforter as though they'd been looked at and set aside. Sabrina recognized a few of the items as having belonged to Steven. She stepped into the room, sat beside Mrs. Starke on the bed and wrapped an arm around her shoulders. "I'm so sorry."

Mrs. Starke sniffed and held out the picture. "I am, too. Sometimes it just overwhelms me."

"Of course it does."

"I think it would help if his murderer was caught. I think then I could find some closure."

"I know that Clay is doing everything he can to make that happen."

Mrs. Starke smiled and patted her hand. She reached into the box and pulled out a picture. "He had this tucked into one of his books."

Sabrina looked at the picture. She and Steven had their heads together. Their expressions were identical. Satisfaction at saving another child. Sabrina blinked back the tears that wanted to surface. "We had gone to pick up a child and take him to an emergency shelter. We stopped at that little diner on Twenty-Sixth and took a selfie." She sighed. "He was determined to save every abused and neglected child he could. We made a great team."

"And now you and Clay have teamed up."

Sabrina gave a soft laugh and handed the picture back to Mrs. Starke. "Yes, I suppose so. He's a lot like Steven, yet very different, too. He's even more driven in some ways."

"Clay's always been that way. He loves his family and this ranch, but he's never wanted to settle here. Steven did."

She wiped her eyes with a crumpled tissue and started to pack up the items. Sabrina stopped her. "Do you mind if I look through them?"

Mrs. Starke shook her head. "Of course not. I want him to be remembered. But I'd better go put in an appearance or I'll have the whole family in here fussing at me for being maudlin."

"I don't think they'd fuss."

"No, probably not."

"I'll be out in a minute. I promise I'll pack everything back up."

Mrs. Starke ran a hand over Sabrina's hair. "You're a sweet child."

Child? Sabrina nearly laughed but supposed she was a child in the woman's eyes. "Thanks."

Mrs. Starke left and Sabrina went through the items one by one, remembering Steven through a haze of tears. Oh, the good times they'd had. Nothing romantic, just good friends. Steven had never indicated he was interested in anything more, but apparently he'd been on the path to healing from the death of his wife. Sabrina knew even had Steven lived, there wouldn't have been anything between them. What she felt for Steven paled in comparison to her growing feelings for his brother.

Clay. What was she going to do about him?

He wanted a life in Nashville. She had no intention of leaving Wrangler's Corner.

Not to mention the whole his-uncle-hated-her thing. If she didn't go away, he was going to withhold his financial help.

Yeah. That was a biggie.

She replaced the items, and her hand hovered over the book. A paperback that she'd loaned Steven. She smiled as she remembered. Steven had had it with him the day he'd died and it had been stuck in the bag with his belongings.

Should she ask for it back or just leave it with his family? She flipped through it and jumped when several photos fell from the pages and into her lap.

She picked one up and gasped. It was fuzzy, as if it had been taken through a dirty window. But two people stood at a stove cooking. She moved to the next picture. Empty boxes, ammonia bottles, empty two liter bottles with plastic hoses. Meth-making materials.

Cold dread settled into the pit of her stomach. She had to talk to Clay immediately. She stood with the box of the rest of the mementos in her hand. Should she take the pictures out to him? Or leave them hidden in the book?

She shoved the pictures back into the box and tucked the book into the back pocket of her jeans. She'd find Mrs. Starke and ask her permission to keep the book. But first she'd find Clay and tell him about the pictures. It was probably better to leave them hidden. She started to place the box on the shelf in the closet, changed her mind and took one of the photos and stuck it in the book. Just in case she needed proof when she talked to Ned and Clay. The rest of the pictures she hid at the bottom of the box. A noise behind her caught her attention.

She whirled and found herself staring into the face of Steven's killer.

SIXTEEN

Clay quietly rounded up a few of Wrangler's Corner's finest, and they all pitched in to look for Stan. Unfortunately to no avail.

They returned to the party but kept an eye out for Stan. The man had left rehab with a goal in mind. To hunt down Sabrina and finish the job? But if it was Stan, why hadn't anyone else seen him?

Clay couldn't spot him in the crowd.

Then again, the man knew how to hide. He knew the hills and the caves better than his own backyard. But around here? Where would he hide?

Seth crutched his way over next to him. "What's got you so on edge?"

Clay told him about the pitchfork incident in the barn with Sabrina.

Seth's jaw tightened. "I'll get my rifle."

"No, just keep an eye out for anyone who looks suspicious."

"Like who?"

"Stan Prescott, for one."

"Where's Sabrina now?"

"In the house with Mom and Amber."

"Mom came outside a few minutes ago and so did Amber and the kids."

"But not Sabrina?"

"No."

"Good. I don't want her out here with Stan on the loose. I'm going to keep searching until I find and arrest him."

"Just to let you know, Mom said Sabrina was a gift. Apparently she cleaned up the kitchen."

Clay gave a slight smile. "Sounds like Sabrina."

Seth raised his eyebrows. "Is it serious between you two?"

"I don't know yet. It's serious enough at this point I want it to be serious."

"Uh-huh."

Clay shrugged. "We've known each other all our lives, and yet I feel like I'm just getting to know her. Although we've spent a lot of time together lately, it's a little soon to jump into serious."

"Right."

"Right." Clay let his gaze rove the property. The partygoers looked happy and well fed. The tables were picked over and the lemonade and tea pitchers drained. And the snow was holding off. "Steven would be proud."

"Yeah. The silent auction seems to be going well, too."

"Wish it was as easy to find a killer as it is to put on a barbecue," Clay grunted.

"Yeah."

Clay made his way to the house, grateful to have Ned's and Lance's help in watching out for Sabrina. If he just kept enough eyes on her, maybe that would be enough to deter the killer.

He stopped when he saw his father standing alone, watching the fun with a sad look in his eyes. "Have you talked to Abe?"

"No."

"What are you going to do about the ranch?"

His father sighed. "There's a horse auction next weekend. I'm going to take the five horses I think will bring the most money and sell them. That'll keep us afloat for a few weeks while I figure out what to do next."

He squeezed his father's shoulder. "We'll work it out. I'm on my way in to check on Sabrina and see if she needs anything."

His dad nodded. "She's a keeper."

Clay shook his head. "That seems to be the general consensus." Lance came from around the corner of the house. "Everything all right?"

Lance shook his head. "Got a call of a domestic disturbance. Ned told me to go check it out."

"Why you? You're not even on duty."

Lance shrugged. "When the boss gives an order..."

"Yeah. Yeah. All right, I'll take over your coverage of the house." He rubbed his hands together. "In fact, I'll just go inside and fill Sabrina in."

"Don't mind spending some time with her, huh?"

Clay gave the man a small smile. "No, that's one thing I don't mind doing."

Sabrina stared at the woman behind the gun. "Krissy? Why?"

"Why what? Why do we want you dead? What exactly is your question?" She shoved Sabrina toward the window. "But it doesn't matter, does it? Out the window."

"What?"

"Out!"

Sabrina took a step backward.

Footsteps sounded in the hall. Krissy snapped a quick glance out, then back to Sabrina. "It's a kid going to the bathroom."

She heard the door shut. Krissy gestured with the gun. "If you're not out the window by the time the little guy comes out, I'll shoot him."

Sabrina flinched. The hard eyes staring at her left her with no doubt the woman would do as she said. She couldn't risk the child's life. Still, she hesitated.

The bathroom door opened, and Krissy stepped

backward, just inside the bedroom door, pistol ready to swing around. "You really want to test me? I'm the one who killed Steven. I also killed Trey. One more won't bother me much."

Sabrina sucked in a deep breath and tried to calm her pounding heart. She would find a way out, but she wouldn't endanger a child. She moved to the window and lifted it. She climbed onto the sill and braced herself to run as soon as her feet hit the ground.

She jumped. Her legs buckled, but she pushed herself up. She took one step. A hard hand over her mouth jolted her to a stop. Time slowed. She could hear the party going on around the corner of the house. She heard someone call her name. Clay?

She saw the big brown car idling and then the strong arms holding her against a broad chest shoved her into the backseat of the vehicle. Time sped back up. Sabrina lashed out with her right foot and caught her attacker on the chin. He cursed and caught her foot. With a hard yank, he pulled her almost back out of the car. Then his fist caught her in the side of the head.

Sabrina now understood what it meant to see stars. Daylight faded. She blinked and went limp, trying to regain her equilibrium, but dizziness hit her hard.

Darkness wanted to take over. She fought it. Felt him duct-taping her ankles. Then her wrists. Terror threatened to smother her. While Clay had been looking for Stan Prescott, Stan Prescott had been looking for her.

And now he had her.

Clay made his way into the house and stopped. Looked around.

"Sabrina?" Nothing. He headed down the hall, checking each room as he went. "Sabrina?" When an entire search of the house turned up empty, panic tried to set in. He rushed back into the kitchen just as his mother stepped inside. "Have you seen Sabrina?"

"I left her in my room looking over Steven's things. She misses him, too."

Clay turned on his heel and made his way back to his parents' bedroom. His mother stayed close behind him. Sabrina had left the box on the bed, neatly packed. Clay stared as emotion wanted to choke him. He pulled the items from the box. Steven's little black comb, two wadded up ten-dollar bills and a few coins.

"Where's the book?" his mother asked.

"What book?"

"It was a paperback. One of the classics. Steven had it in his coat pocket when he was killed."

"And it's gone now. Are you sure it was in here?" She made a sound of disgust. "Of course I'm sure. I just saw it." She frowned. "Why would Sabrina take it?"

"Maybe she loaned it to him. She said they often swapped books back and forth."

"But would she just take it without telling me? That doesn't sound like her."

"No," Clay agreed as fear clamped down on him. "No, it doesn't." He bolted from the room, through the kitchen and out the front door. He looked around and found Ned talking to Aaron. "Have you guys seen Sabrina?"

"No," Ned said. "Have you seen Krissy? Lance asked me to let her know her brother called and her mother's taken a turn for the worse. I was just telling Aaron I may go see if there's anything I can do to help."

"I saw Krissy in the kitchen with Sabrina not too long ago. She said she saw Stan Prescott hovering nearby. Any chance you've spotted him?"

"No." Aaron grimaced. "He knows better than to show his face around here."

"Maybe not."

Clay raced back to the house and into his parents' bedroom, looking for some kind of clue. Sabrina had last been seen here. But his search turned up nothing.

He called her cell phone, and it went straight to voice mail.

"Clay? I'm getting ready to leave, but what's going on?" Ned asked from behind him.

He turned. "Sabrina's missing. Can you ping her phone?"

Ned didn't stop to ask questions, just got on his phone to get the deed done.

Clay ran back out and questioned each guest, asking the same question over and over. "Have you seen Sabrina?"

Each time he got a negative answer, his despair deepened.

Until Tony Zellis pulled on his sleeve. "I saw her. They put her in that car."

Clay knelt, doing his best to keep his desperation under control. "What car, son?"

"The big brown one."

"Who put her in the car?"

"The lady. And the man. I was going to tell her to stop, but they left before I could."

A lady?

A big brown car?

"They put her in, you said. Was she walking or were they carrying her?"

"She was walking kind of funny. Like my mom does sometimes when she drinks a lot. Ms. Sabrina came out of the window and the man helped her down."

Clay pinched the bridge of his nose. "Came out of the window?"

"Uh-huh. And the man grabbed her, and the lady climbed out after her."

Think, man. "What did the man look like?"

Tony shrugged. "A man." He frowned. "Is Ms. Sabrina going to be okay?"

"Yes." Clay forced a smile. "If I have anything to say about it, she will be."

"Okay. Good. I like her."

"Yeah," Clay whispered. "Me, too."

Who had a big brown car? What lady and what man? He looked around, trying to see who was missing, but there were at least sixty people mingling in the yard, coming and going from the house, and gathered around the bonfire. Unless he called for a head count, he wasn't going to be able to figure it out.

Had someone helped Stan snatch Sabrina with the party going on?

A cold ball of fear formed in his gut. Surely not. He moved to the back of the house. Stan Prescott stood at the edge of the trees, right where Krissy had said she'd spotted him earlier. Clay raced toward the man. "Stan!"

Stan simply looked at him, stood still and lifted his hands in the air in a gesture of surrender. Clay pulled his weapon and held it on the man. "Where's Sabrina?"

Stan didn't speak. Clay moved closer. Stan stepped back into the woods. "Be still! Don't move!"

Clay held his gun steady and reached for his phone, keeping his eyes on the man who might know something about Sabrina.

At the edge of the woods, he pressed the button that would bring backup.

Stan dropped his hands. Clay tensed. "Put them back up, Stan."

Lightning pain hit the back of his head. His vision went white. Then black.

Sabrina's head pounded, and fear nauseated her. She had done away with her sling yesterday afternoon. Working in the barn had stretched the healing area, and it had been sore this morning. With her wrists bound behind her back, pain pulsed a steady beat in the wounded area. Finding a more comfortable position was impossible. With her feet also duct-taped together, she had very limited movement. Her cheek hurt, and her ears still rang. Memory returned in fragments. Stan had punched her. She'd blacked out at some point.

She let her senses take in all the information she could process. A metal floor beneath her. That meant she was no longer in the brown car.

So where was she?

An idling engine. A metal floor. Darkness, but she could see the snow falling through two windows toward the back of the vehicle. She figured she'd been transferred to a van. Time had passed but not too much, as it was still light outside.

So now she was tied up and scared to death.

Krissy and Stan had disappeared without a word a short while ago. Sabrina knew it was now or never. She tugged and struggled and cried out until she was breathless. Her head throbbed. Panting, she wiped her tears on her shoulder. "Oh, Lord, please, help me."

The back of the van opened, spilling sunlight into the cavernous interior. Another body landed next to her. Sabrina gasped and shrank away.

Then realized who it was. "Clay!"

The doors slammed shut once again.

Sabrina scooted on her hip closer to Clay. He lay so still, so quiet. Was he even alive? She shivered, her teeth chattering. She curled next to his warmth. The front doors opened, and the two criminals climbed in. The van rumbled to life. "Clay," she whispered. "Can you hear me?"

Sabrina could see the snowflakes coming down fast and furious through the back windows, but soon the sun would disappear and they would be plunged into darkness.

Heat from the front started to penetrate to the back, and her shivers eased, but each jolt over the rough ground slammed her against the floor, sending shards of agony through her injured shoulder.

She had a feeling any healing that had taken place had just been reversed.

She noticed Clay having a hard time, too. Every time they hit a bump, his head knocked the metal floor. Ignoring her own discomfort, she winced and maneuvered herself against him, trying to roll him next to the wall of the van without attracting the attention of those up front.

Finally, she had him trapped between her body and the side of the van. It made the bouncing a bit more bearable.

And allowed her to tune in to the conversation of the two in the front.

"...told you this was a bad idea," Stan said.

"Shut up and drive."

"Why am I listening to you?" The van swerved, then jerked back into the lane. Sabrina grimaced and tried to move with it.

"Because you're a fool if you don't," Krissy said, her voice so low and lethal that Sabrina flinched and waited for the gunshot that would end Stan's life.

When it didn't come, Sabrina ignored her massive discomfort and tried to nudge Clay awake again. His unresponsiveness worried her. How hard had Stan hit him? "Clay," she whispered.

"Quit whining and tell me if you got the pictures," Krissy snapped.

"I'll get them when we get to the cave. I was

watching her from the window. She's got them in that book in her back pocket."

"Why didn't you grab them when you tossed her in the van?" Outrage vibrated in Krissy's voice.

"Because I was too busy trying to figure how to get Clay Starke, in case you didn't notice. I could hear him coming and thanks to my quick thinking, he's not going to be a problem anymore." He snorted. "You're a piece of work, aren't you?"

Krissy huffed. "Just drive."

"Oh, I'm driving, all right." The menace in Stan's voice sent chills up Sabrina's spine. She wasn't sure which person scared her more.

"So they were in the book after all," Krissy mused after about a minute of silence. "Jordan told the truth."

"Looks like."

"Maybe it's a good thing we didn't kill her. We'd still be looking for those pictures if she'd died. This way we have the pictures and can make her and Clay's death look like an accident." Krissy paused. "And once we're done with them, I've got to get back and take care of that kid. He saw us put Sabrina in the car."

"What kid?"

"Tony Zellis."

"Jordan's little brother?"

"Yes. I would have grabbed him, but he ran off and you were fighting a losing battle with Sabrina."

"I wasn't losing."

"Whatever. I can't let that kid live now. He might not know my name, but as soon as he sees me again, he'll be able to point at me and say, 'That's the lady who put Sabrina in the car.'" She blew out a harsh breath. "This is getting messier and messier."

"Exactly. So how do you plan to make their deaths look like an accident when the kid is running around telling people she was kidnapped?"

"I don't know!" she screeched. "I'll just have to think of something, won't I?"

"Well, if Jordan had just kept his mouth shut, none of this would have happened."

"Yeah, well, unfortunately, Jordan has a big mouth. One even his best friend couldn't shut up."

Silence reigned in the front. Then Krissy spoke again. "If he had just followed the plan at your trailer, all of this would have been unnecessary."

"Plan? What plan?"

"The plan to make it look like Jordan turned against everyone and killed them. And then turned the gun on himself and ended it all."

Stan seemed to think about that. Then he spoke. "I've never killed a kid before."

"Well, neither have I, but if comes down to him or me, it's not going to be me. And now that we have the pictures, we don't need Jordan."

"You've killed a kid. You killed Trey."

"He doesn't count. He was killing himself with the drugs anyway. I just helped the inevitable happen a little faster."

"I'll fill the boss in on everything after we dump these two."

Sabrina stilled. Boss?

The two fell quiet once again, and a violent shiver racked her, the chill having nothing to do with the temperature outside.

SEVENTEEN

Clay groaned and wished dire things upon the people using the jackhammer on his skull. A roar filled his ears and the ground shook…and rocked. His head throbbed, and his stomach lurched.

He rolled and had to bite down on the scream that wanted to escape him. Blackness covered him once again.

"Clay?"

The whisper ricocheted through him. He blinked and wished he hadn't.

"Clay? Wake up."

Sabrina. He opened his eyes again and stared into darkness. Panic gripped him. Was he blind? He lifted a hand to his head. His fingers came away wet. Blood, he figured. "Where are we?" he rasped.

A sob reached him. "Oh, Clay, I was so scared you weren't going to wake up. Are you okay?"

"I think I'm blind. I can't see."

"You're not blind. We're trapped in one of the caves. They set off dynamite or something and closed off the entrance." She paused. "And exit, I'm afraid."

A shiver racked him. Fortunately, he had his heavy Sherpa coat on. Not so fortunately, he didn't have his gloves on. His hands felt frozen. The throbbing in his head had eased only slightly, and the nausea churning didn't bode well.

"Are you okay?"

"My hands and feet are duct-taped together. Can you get me loose?"

Remorse hit him. "Why didn't you say so?" The blow to his head had scrambled his brain. Keeping his head as still as possible, he moved toward her. For a moment he thought he might black out. He rested his head against the cold cave floor. "Hang on a second."

He heard her scooting toward him. "Just stay there. I'll come to you." More scraping and he felt her next to him. He reached out and felt her shoulder. He slid a hand down her arm and found the tape.

"My hands are so cold I'm not sure how fast I'll be."

"Well, we need to hurry and get out of here. They're going to kill Tony. Not only that, I didn't bring all the pictures with me. They'll go back to the ranch to find them."

Clay sucked in a breath. He winced. "Explain while I work on this."

Sabrina filled him in on the conversation she'd overheard. "But there's another thing that worries me."

"What's that?"

"They didn't sound like they were working alone. They referred to someone as 'boss.'"

Clay tugged and felt a strip loosen. He unwrapped and unwound until finally her hands fell free. She gasped, and he reached up to rub her arms. "Get the circulation going."

"Oh, wow. That hurt."

"Swing your feet around here."

"I can do it. You rest a minute."

He didn't argue. Couldn't. His head swam, and he was losing the battle with the nausea.

Being as still as possible for the next several minutes restored him slightly. "I'd kill for an aspirin."

"Or four?"

"Exactly."

"I know what you mean."

"Did they hurt you?" He reached out to find her hand.

She squeezed his fingers. "I'm fine. But we need to get out of here."

"It would help if we had some light. Do you know what cave we're in?"

"No."

A scraping sound found his ears. He paused. "You hear that?"

"Yes," she whispered. "What could it be?"

"Bats, I'm guessing."

"Ew. Please tell me no." She pressed closer to him.

He heard more movement from up above. "Just ignore them." He took a deep breath and pulled himself into a sitting position, then had to stop and rest for a minute. The feel of her next to him helped, not necessarily physically, but her nearness gave him the emotional motivation to overcome his weakness and get her out of the cave. He refused to let her die here. And as soon as his head quit spinning, he'd get started on a plan of action.

"I'm scared, Clay," she whispered.

He wrapped an arm around her shoulders. "We'll work on getting out of here in just a sec." There wasn't any way he could move at the moment. *Please, God, give me strength.* "You know when you asked me about Bryce England back at the diner?"

She laid her head on his shoulder. "Yes."

"Bryce was one of the bullies who targeted my sister when she was in high school."

"Oh."

"I didn't burn down his house, though." The dizziness started to ease, and he leaned his head back against the wall of the cave. She clasped his hand in hers. At least he thought she did. His were so cold he almost felt numb.

"What happened?"

"Steven and I went over to confront him, to tell him to leave Amber alone. Bryce's parents were gone and, being teenagers, we decided that was the perfect time to do a little bullying of our own."

"Uh-oh."

"Yes." He shifted and grunted at the shaft of pain that shot through the back and base of his skull. Her hand tightened around his. "Bryce and his brother had built a bonfire out back. Steven and I walked up and said our piece. Bryce simply laughed at us and started throwing pieces of burning wood at us. Steven punched him pretty good one time. His brother jumped me, and we all went at it. None of us noticed that one of the burning pieces of wood had caught the patio carpet on fire."

He felt tremors race through Sabrina and lifted his head, testing it. It hurt, but he wasn't dizzy. A small improvement, but he'd take it.

"And the fire reached the house?" she asked.

"Yes. From the outdoor carpet to the wood railing. By the time the flames caught our attention, it was too late. Bryce ran screaming into the house. Steven and I went after him. Steven found him and pulled him out." He swallowed, his dry throat aching. "I called 911. By the time it was all over and done with, Bryce and his brother blamed me."

"But not Steven?"

He shrugged and then winced as he made a mental note not to move. Yet. "No. I guess he figured he owed Steven for pulling him out, but he sure made my life miserable with his accusations. Steven tried to defend me, but everyone just assumed it was because he was my brother."

"But they couldn't prove anything, because you didn't do anything, right?"

"Right. My name was just dragged through the mud for a while. People still remember."

"I remember some of that. Lily seemed to think it was true, and I didn't know what to believe."

"Well, now you know. We're going to get out of here. Where's the entrance?"

He heard her move.

And gasp.

"What is it?"

"We're not the only ones in here."

Sabrina shuddered as she reached out a hand to touch the body she'd just rolled into.

"Who is it?"

"I don't know," she whispered. She ran her hands up and found the person's throat. A faint pulse beat beneath her fingers. "He's alive, though."

"Who is it?"

"I don't know. I can't tell."

"All right, let's get busy getting out of here."

"But how?"

"I guess we dig unless you've got a better idea. We've got to get to my family. I refuse to let these people win."

Sabrina made her way to the blocked entrance of the cave. Debris, small and large, made her travel difficult, but she pushed aside the rocks, pulling and shoving. Clay joined her. After what seemed like hours, she clutched her bleeding hands and leaned her head against the rocks. "This is hopeless."

"No, it's not," Clay said. "Look." Excitement and relief filled her at the faint beam of light seeping through a crack in the rock wall.

Clay dug faster, and she added her own efforts.

Until a noise on the other side stopped them. Her shivering had ceased, the exertion causing a sweat to break across her forehead. "Did you hear that?"

"Yes." Clay leaned toward the faint light. "Hello! We're trapped! Get help!"

Rocks tumbled from the other side. "Just dig. There's a weak spot here—it's not very thick. I've been digging since they left."

"Jordan?" Sabrina nearly went to her knees. Dizzy with relief, she sent up a prayer of thanks.

More rocks tumbled on the other side.

"Yeah. They had C4 planted in the cave. They were planning this all along, I guess. I found some of the C4 and removed it, but obviously I didn't get it all. At least I got enough that it didn't bring the whole cave down on top of you." He finished the sentence on a grunt as more debris fell away from the opening. "Which is what I think they were hoping for."

The sliver of light widened. She turned to find Clay beside her digging. Together they worked in silence until the sliver became a hole. Hands bleeding and sore, she didn't let up. She couldn't. She had to get to the house.

The hole grew bigger, and Clay paused, gasping. He rested his head against the cool wall and she touched his cheek. "Just a little more."

"Yeah." His slanted glance went to the hole. "You could slip through there now."

"I'm not going until it's big enough for you to crawl through, too." She thought she might have to help him. Jordan could pull, and she could push on her end.

He shoved out of his jacket and tossed it through the opening.

With another five minutes of digging, the hole was big enough for Clay. And whoever was in the cave with them.

She moved and felt the man's pulse. "Still beating. Let's get him out." She moved to the hole. "Jordan?"

"Yes?"

"We have someone else in here. Clay can't pick

him up. I need you to crawl through the hole so I can hand you his arms. You'll have to pull him out while I push from this end, okay?"

"Okay."

She saw Jordan's face, and Clay lifted the man's arms. Jordan grasped them. Clay was able to push while Jordan pulled and finally, they had him on the other side.

She turned to Clay. "Go."

"No way. You first."

"Clay, you're hurt. I might have to help push you through. Please. Go." She looked at the exit. "I might need you to pull me through anyway."

He gave her a tender smile. "Trying to save my pride, huh?"

"Doesn't matter, it's true. Now go."

Clay climbed through. Jordan helped from his end. Sabrina reached up to push on the heels of his boots. The bats behind her put up a screeching protest at the light now invading their territory. She shuddered. Clay's feet disappeared.

"Come on, Sabrina." She saw his battered face in the opening. She grasped the edges and wiggled into the hole. Hands clamped around her wrists and within seconds, she stood before a swaying Clay and a ragged-looking Jordan Zellis. She hugged the thin teenager. "I'm so glad you're alive."

"Well, I almost wasn't."

"Where have you been? What happened to your

face?" His right eye was almost swollen shut. His cracked upper lip sported a scab and he had nasty bruises under both cheeks.

"I've been tied up in a barn. I just managed to get away a few hours ago." He touched his face. "You might say I got beat up when I wouldn't tell them what I knew."

"Why didn't they just kill you?"

"Because I knew where the pictures were."

"The ones in the book."

"Right."

She dropped beside the man who'd been in the cave with them. "It's Lance," she whispered. "Krissy's husband."

Clay hit the ground beside her. He patted his friend's face, felt his pulse. "Hey, man, can you hear me?"

Nothing.

"He needs a doctor." Sabrina ran her hands down the man's chest and side and stopped when she felt a wetness. She held her hand up. "I think he's been shot." She cleaned her hand in the snow and then dried it on her jeans while sending up a silent prayer for Lance.

Clay rubbed his temple. "All right. We're going to have to move pretty fast."

"We can't just leave him here. He'll die." Clay bit his lip and swayed. Sabrina caught his arm. "And you're in no shape to go anywhere."

"I'll be all right. I wasn't planning to leave him here, but we can't carry him. Let me think a minute." He closed his eyes. When he opened them, he said, "He's got his heavy down coat on and his gloves. He'll be warm enough." He looked at the teen. "You'll have to stay with him."

"No way. I'm going to find my brother and sister."

"We're going to take care of them," Clay said. "But we can't leave Lance alone, and we can't take him with us. Once we get to a phone, help should be here within the hour."

Jordan hesitated. "What if he dies? Everyone will blame me."

"No. Just do your best, son. But the longer we stand here, the longer it's going to take for Lance to get his help."

Jordan finally agreed.

"I'm going to patch him up as best I can, but you may have to lie next to him and share your body warmth."

Jordan nodded. "I'll do it."

Clay started working on Lance.

"Who had you?" Sabrina asked.

"Krissy Goode and that Stan Prescott. They wanted to know where the pictures were."

"The pictures in the book?"

He started. "Yes, you found them?"

"I did."

"I gave them to Steven. I saw him put them in the book, but I didn't know what happened to them after he died." Shame flooded his face. "I'm sorry I lured you out to the trailer. The voice on the phone said it was a joke and she'd give me fifty bucks. I now think it was Krissy who called me. But when I saw Steven's wallet, I knew something wasn't right."

"Why didn't you tell me about Krissy when you called to warn me?"

"I didn't know she was involved in anything when I called you. I had watched that meth lab for a long time and she was only there once or twice, but I never saw her face and in the pictures, she's kind of blurry. *She's* the one who recognized herself." He frowned. "But I don't think she was worried so much about herself as she was the other people I'd caught coming and going. They're her customers and if they find out they got photographed, they'll kill her." He sighed. "I'm really sorry."

Sabrina hadn't had any trouble recognizing Krissy in the pictures. "Don't beat yourself up about it—I'm fine." She glanced down at herself. "Dirty, a little bloody, but very happy to be alive." She stepped out of the cave and looked around. A world of white greeted her. Dread filled her even as the cold hit her. She shivered and tucked her bloodied, bruised hands into her jeans pockets. She hadn't had on a coat when Krissy had forced her out the window.

Clay dropped his coat over her shoulders as though he could read her mind. The instant warmth felt blissful. The instant guilt didn't. "I can't take this, Clay. You're hurt." She took the coat off and tried to give it back to him. He simply stared at her. He wasn't going to take the coat back. Fine. She wrapped it around herself and huddled into it. When he dropped beside Lance to check him over one more time, Sabrina asked Jordan, "Why did Krissy and Stan come after me?"

Jordan dropped his gaze. "Because of me. Or rather my pictures." He gulped. "Steven was like a dad to me. He pulled me out of trouble one day and gave me an option. Straighten up or go to jail. Asked me what my dreams were and then bought me a camera. I'd never really had anyone care about what I did, so when it looked like Steven was different, I was determined to straighten up. I had the big idea that I could become a cop like him, so I decided to bust the meth ring he was looking for. I was at the meth lab, not Stan's trailer but another one. Someone saw me taking pictures and came after me. I'd managed to get away, but I'd been lying low. Trey started asking me questions about why I wasn't around so much and what I was doing. When I told him, he laughed and told me I was a loser. Then not too long after that, he was all buddy-buddy again."

"To keep your trust and see what you knew?"

"Yes. Apparently."

Sabrina exchanged a glance with Clay. She thought he looked ready to keel over. He'd been knocked in the head hard twice in a very short period of time. That couldn't be good. "I saw the pictures, Jordan," she said. "They had just Krissy in them and a couple of other people at the meth lab. There weren't any of me. Why would they come after me?"

"There weren't any *printed* pictures of you. Krissy found the ones on the camera. The ones of you and Steven exchanging the book. I saw you guys at the café sitting outside and I snapped a picture. I didn't have one of him...." He shrugged. "I looked up to Steven," he whispered. "He was my hero." He cleared his throat. "Anyway, when she saw the picture, she thought you had it." He slapped his head. "If only I hadn't said they were in the book. If I'd just said I burned them or gave them to someone, they wouldn't have come after you."

"But they would have killed you."

"Probably."

EIGHTEEN

Clay listened to Jordan talk even while he focused on his friend. The dizziness had mostly passed, but the stabbing headache nearly blinded him. Lance lay still and quiet. Did he know about Krissy? Had he known what his wife was doing? That she was a murderer?

Clay couldn't see it.

She'd left him to die in the cave, too.

He made a mental note to make sure they came back and gathered up the C4 Jordan had removed from the cave.

Assuming everything resolved in a favorable way.

As he finished patching up Lance, Clay offered up a heartfelt prayer. *God, I haven't relied on You much lately. Been kind of mad at You, to be honest. You let them kill Steven, and that's been hard to deal with. But...I'm sorry. I'm not one for hit-and-run prayers though, so I figure it's just better not to ask for anything rather than constantly ask when I'm not giving anything back.* Weakness wanted to take over, but Clay refused to give in. He thought of his mother and how she continued to be faithful and trust in God even in her grief. *I'm asking now, God, that You spare my family and those innocent children. Don't let Lance die. And help me keep my feet under me when we start moving.*

Would God listen?

Yes. Clay had no doubt He would.

Would He answer the way Clay wanted?

That remained to be seen, but Clay would go forward as though He would.

He felt Lance's pulse once more. "Hang in there, buddy," he whispered, praying his friend could hear him. He was satisfied he'd done everything he could do. Now it was up to God—and Clay, who had to get him some help.

He tuned back in to what Jordan and Sabrina were talking about as he used Lance's belt to secure the makeshift bandage over his friend's side.

"So you're saying they saw the picture of me and Steven exchanging the book. But I was giving it to him, not the other way around." Clay didn't have to look at her to hear the frown in her voice.

"Yeah, but they didn't know that. And I had told them that the pictures were in the book before they saw the one with you and Steven." He sighed. "I didn't know they'd find those pictures on my camera, make the assumption you had the book and come after you. I thought they'd just look for the book. When I realized they thought *you* had it, I tried to tell them you didn't, but they didn't believe me." He walked a few more steps, then looked sideways at her. "Krissy killed Trey and Steven, didn't she?"

"Yes."

Tears filled the boy's eyes. "Yeah." He swiped his free hand across his face. "Well, Trey turned out to be not such a great friend anyway, didn't he?"

Sabrina squeezed his hand, then let go. "I overheard one of them say something about a 'boss.' Do you know who that could be?"

Jordan shrugged and shook his head. "No. Sorry."

Clay stood. Dizziness hit him, and he closed his eyes to let it and the nausea pass. He swayed, and Sabrina placed a hand on his arm. "Is Lance going to be okay?"

"I don't know. I've done the best I can to stop the bleeding and bind the wound. My T-shirt isn't exactly sanitary, but I figure it's better than letting him bleed out. He needs medical help pretty fast."

"Then we need to figure out what we're going to do," Sabrina said.

"Clay?" Lance whispered.

Clay felt relief sweep him. "Lance, you're awake."

"The pain's sort of interrupting my nap," he rasped.

"Can you walk?" Clay asked as he dropped beside his friend again.

"Maybe. With some help."

"The bullet went straight through. I couldn't tell if it hit anything terribly important on its way out."

"I guess the fact that I'm still alive says maybe not."

"Who shot you?" Jordan asked.

Lance's pained face doubled. "Not sure." He looked at Clay. "There wasn't any domestic disturbance. When I got to the address, I stepped out of my car and got hit. Next thing I know, you're bending over me and I feel like someone's run a hot poker through my side."

Clay and Jordan helped Lance to his feet. The man groaned but stayed upright.

"Where's the nearest phone?" Sabrina asked.

"The Nelsons' convenience store is about a mile ahead," Clay said. "I worked there one summer when I was in high school." The snow wasn't deep. Yet. But it was cold.

"If there's any power," Jordan muttered. He glanced around. "Look at the ice on the trees."

Clay looked at Jordan, then back at Lance. "We need to get Lance help and we need to get to a phone to call Ned as soon as possible." His brow furrowed. "I'd send Jordan to call for help while I head for the ranch, but that's going to take him a while and I don't want to leave Lance here by himself."

"You can leave me. I'll be all right."

"No way," Clay said.

"I could stay with him," Sabrina said. "But I'm not sure you'll make it to the ranch by yourself. What if you pass out or something?"

Clay closed his eyes, having a hard time getting his brain to work. "And I don't think I can help Lance by myself. I need Jordan." He pressed a hand to his head and looked at the three of them. "I think our best plan is to stay together." He glanced at his watch, then the darkening sky. "I would also say the party at the ranch is probably winding down and time is of the essence, so we need to go."

Lance grunted. "What's the deal? Why are you guys up here?"

Lance didn't appear to know anything about his wife's duplicity. "You're not going to want to hear the truth."

His friend frowned. "About?"

Clay sucked in a deep breath and caught Sabrina's frown and slight shake of her head. "Looks like Stan Prescott and a partner are behind the meth lab. But we're not going to worry about that now. We need to get you some help." Clay and Jordan helped Lance to his feet and took a few tentative steps. "You going to make it?" he asked Lance.

"Guess we'll find out."

The snow continued to fall as Sabrina watched the three men start walking. She looked at Jordan. Might as well ask the question she knew was foremost on Clay's mind. "What happened the day Steven died?"

"I had called Steven and told him I had evidence about a meth lab. Steven said he'd come get the evidence."

"Was that your pipe in your room?" She told him about seeing it the day she went to visit him and his siblings.

"No way. I was done with that stuff. Trey gave it to me that day. I was going to throw it out, then thought it might be used for evidence. Trey was working with Krissy—"

"Krissy?" Lance stumbled to a stop. Jordan and Clay held him upright. "What are you talking about?"

Sabrina grimaced. "Krissy is Stan's partner," she told him quietly.

Lance swayed. "No way. I don't believe it." He turned pained eyes on Sabrina. "Why would you say that?"

"Because it's true. I found evidence."

"What kind?"

She told him, and he fell silent, his expression shattered. Sabrina's heart broke for the man.

Jordan's gaze flitted between her and Lance. Lance pinned Jordan with a look. "Go ahead and finish what you were saying about Trey and Krissy working together. I want to hear it all."

Jordan bit his lip, then said, "I didn't know it until later when they had me tied up in the barn and were talking about stuff. I even asked them questions and they were willing to fill me in." He shuddered. "Even laughed while they told me stuff." Terror crossed his face at the memory and Sabrina wanted to comfort him. "Before all that, I told Trey I was going to tell Steven about the meth lab. I told him I didn't know who all was involved, but I had pictures." He shifted Lance's weight. Lance groaned but didn't seem to have the strength to do more. Sabrina could tell he was getting weaker by the step. She wanted to lend her support but was afraid she'd just get in the way.

Jordan said, "Trey came over just before Steven got to the house."

Lance groaned again and fell to his knees. Clay landed beside him and put his head in his hands. Jordan kept a tight grip on Lance to keep him from landing face-first in the snow. Sabrina grabbed him by the upper arms and lowered him gently to the ground.

She knew the basics of first aid thanks to her

social work training. She placed her fingers on Lance's wrist. His pulse beat faint and unsteady. How was he even still conscious? "Are you going to be able to make it?" she asked softly.

"The spirit is willing, but I'm afraid I may pass out." His erratic breathing worried her, and Clay's obvious weakness scared her. She tried not to worry about what might be happening at the Starke house. As long as there were still guests there, the family and the children should be all right. Krissy and Stan would bide their time, striking when they thought they wouldn't get caught. The thought wasn't much comfort. The time was passing quickly, and the temperature was dropping fast.

"Help me up," Lance said. "We can't stop now."

Clay got to his feet and pulled Lance's arm across his broad shoulders while Jordan did the same on the other side. Sabrina felt helpless. "What can I do?"

"Just stay close in case you have to catch one of us," Clay muttered.

Sabrina didn't think he was joking.

As they started off again, Jordan said, "When Trey showed up at the house, Steven hadn't gotten there yet. Trey asked me if I still planned on talking to Steven. I said yeah, so when Steven got there, I told him everything and I gave him the pictures of the meth lab. He put them in the book he had in his pocket. Then Trey said he had to be somewhere and needed a ride. He suggested Steven take him while they talked."

"He didn't have his truck?" Clay asked. Sabrina heard the thin thread of pain in his voice.

"No. I'd picked him up on my motorcycle. Steven and Trey got in his car and left. I know Steven dropped Trey off because Steven called and told me he had to take Trey somewhere the next day and couldn't meet me." He gnawed on a fingernail and shook his head. "I think Trey must have set him up, told someone—probably Krissy—and she killed him," he whispered. "I heard he was dead and I couldn't believe it. I tried to find Trey but he was missing." They were all listening to Jordan talk. Sabrina thought his story helped propel them onward through the falling snow, through the fatigue and the desire to just sit down and give up.

Lance stumbled against Clay, who almost lost his balance. She thought Clay looked even more pale than he had five minutes ago. "Are you all right? Do we need to stop for a minute?"

"I'm not feeling great, but I'll make it." Anxiety and worry for his family and the children were plainly etched into his handsome features. Sabrina knew exactly how he felt.

On the next step, Clay tripped, caught himself and paused, swaying, his grip on Lance never lessening. Lance didn't make a sound, just cringed. She wasn't sure how he was staying vertical. Sabrina grabbed Lance's arm and put it over her shoulders. "Let me do this for a while. You definitely have a concussion."

"No doubt about it, but there's nothing to do about it until we make sure my family and the kids are safe." Clay frowned at her. "He's too heavy for you."

"I'll manage."

Sabrina nodded and stepped forward, ignoring Clay's weak protest. Lance's weight almost took her to the ground. Jordan must have sensed her predicament, because he shifted the man so that Lance leaned more heavily against him. Jordan continued his story. "She killed Steven. I thought at first it was Stan because he had Steven's wallet in the trailer, but when they had me tied up in the barn, they talked in front of me." He swallowed hard. "I know it's because they planned to kill me as soon as they got what they needed from me."

"How long have they had you?"

"Since the day I called you at the trailer. Stan came after me and found me. He took me to Krissy and they tied me up and tried to get me to tell them what I knew. The only reason they didn't kill me right away is because they thought I knew more than I did." He cleared his throat and shivered, his voice growing hoarse. "And I let them think that. They kept asking me who knew about the meth lab and who had I shown the pictures to. They knocked me out a couple of times trying to get me to talk."

Clay started walking again, shoulders hunched against the elements. Sabrina felt guilty for keeping his coat but knew he'd rather her wear it if she was cold. His selflessness touched her. Made her appreciate the feeling of being cared for as never before. Her grandmother loved her, of course, but Sabrina figured she was supposed to.

A sharp crack cut through the air, and a puff of white shot up in front of her. She flinched, and Clay hollered, "Get down! Get down!" He came up next to them and shoved her toward the tree line. "Get behind a tree, now! Jordan, get a tight grip and run!"

Confused but not questioning his order, she shot off the trail and into the woods. She heard the men behind her and heard another loud pop. "Go, Sabrina," Clay panted. "Go deeper into the woods. Find a thick copse of trees."

Someone had discovered they hadn't died in the cave and was shooting at them again. Her breath caught in her throat, and she uttered a desperate prayer. *Lord, let this nightmare end. Please let everything work out right so we can get on with our lives. And if you could see a way for Clay and me... well...you know what I'm praying for.*

They moved fast, leaving a trail to follow but hopefully putting enough trees between them and the shooter. The snow came heavier and harder, and Sabrina felt true fear shake her insides.

They finally slowed when no more shots came. Jordan separated from Clay and Lance and leaned against the nearest tree, clutching his side.

"Are you hurt?" Sabrina ran to him and pulled his hand away. No blood.

Jordan shook his head. "No. A cramp."

Relief filled her. She turned back to Lance and Clay. "What about you two?"

"No new bullet wounds, thankfully," Clay said. "But all that rushing caused Lance's wound to start bleeding again." He held his friend, who was just barely conscious.

"The convenience store is just ahead," Clay said. "Jordan, can you run as fast as you can and call for an ambulance? You'll have to stay behind the cover of the trees. Fortunately, the store backs up to the woods. You can jump over the concrete wall and be inside faster than we'll be able to move together. It'll be locked, but there should be a key in a small magnetic holder under the mailbox. Get help on the way."

"Sure." He took off, careful to move from tree to tree. Sabrina held her breath and when no more shots came, sent up a silent thank-you. "How did you know where the key would be?"

"I used to work there when I was in high school. I'm just praying it's still there."

Clay caught Lance. He felt his pulse. "He's passed out. His pulse feels weaker."

"It wasn't that strong to begin with. I'm really worried about him."

"I'm worried about all of us." He held Lance against him. Sabrina thought the color in Clay's face looked a bit better. He said, "Can we keep going? See if we can get him into the store?"

"Yes. Of course."

It wasn't easy, but they made it to the back entrance, using the trees for cover, just as Jordan came rushing out. "The phone's dead."

NINETEEN

Clay helped his friend stretch out on the floor. The mom-and-pop convenience store was warm enough but cooling rapidly. "The power hasn't been off long. See if you can find a kerosene heater and some propane."

Jordan held up the cordless phone. "These things work great as long as you have electricity."

"The Nelsons own this place," Clay said. "They have cell phones, so they probably don't worry about it if the power goes out." He sighed. "Great."

"Lance is unconscious?" Sabrina asked.

Clay nodded. "Yeah. And we've got a shooter out there who may have figured out where we were heading. But the shots were coming from behind us. That's one of the reasons I sent Jordan running ahead. That and it was a good idea to get to a phone as fast as possible."

"Good thinking."

"But now…I don't know who's shooting. I'm

assuming it's Krissy or Stan, but it could be whoever the boss is."

"So what do we do? If we go out there, we could
get shot. If we stay here, your family and the kids
could die."

Clay's head pounded with the decisions. Stay
or go? Jordan had found a heater and had it hum-
ming along.

"There's no choice," Sabrina said. "We have to
go—you realize that, right?"

He looked at her. "That's an open field out there."

She went to the window. "And the snow is coming down pretty hard."

She bit her lip and he reached out to cup her
chin. "Are you praying?"

"With every breath."

He gave her a light kiss on her lips. "Me, too.
I want to get this settled. I want the good guys to
win and the bad guys to be in jail. Then I want to
talk about us."

She nodded. "I'd like that, too." Her brows
dipped. "But what about your family? Your uncle
Abe and how he feels about me?"

"Uncle Abe doesn't control me or my family,
Sabrina."

"But the money for the ranch—"

He placed a finger over her lips. "Will you trust
me?"

She gave a slow nod. "Good." He released her

and walked to the window. "It's snowing like crazy, but this could work in our favor."

"So we go?"

Clay sucked in a deep breath. "Well, I go. Jordan, you and Sabrina are going to have to stay here with Lance." He walked over to the register and wrote a note to the Nelsons. Then he grabbed a bottle of ibuprofen and downed four. Next he grabbed a ginger ale and handed it to Jordan. "Try and get Lance to drink this. It's not exactly an IV drip, but he needs fluids. Write down whatever you use, and I'll make sure the Nelsons get paid for it."

Jordan nodded, then shook his head. "I want to make sure Tony and Maria are safe."

"And I need you to do this for…" Clay swallowed hard.

"For?"

"For Steven, Jordan. Do it for Steven. I'm going to go down that hill and put his killers in jail. I need you to take care of Lance."

Clay thought the teen would refuse at first, but then he nodded. "Please don't let anything happen to them."

"I'm going with you," Sabrina said.

Clay frowned. "It's quite a hike, and there's a guy with a rifle out there."

"We can stay close to the tree line. It's the long

way, of course, but it'll take us right to the Updike farm. They'll have a phone we can use."

"Sabrina—"

"I'm going. If you pass out and we're back here, you could freeze to death out there and there wouldn't be anyone else to go for help. No way. I'm going with you."

He gave a reluctant nod and touched the lump on his head. At least his mind seemed to be a little less foggy. "I'm feeling better, but… Fine. You're probably right."

Jordan sat on the floor beside Lance, trying to get the man to drink. Lance blinked, took a sip, then passed out again. Clay clapped him on the shoulder. "Just keep trying, okay?"

"Sure. Be careful."

Clay grabbed the heaviest coat he could find on the clothing rack, two scarves, two hats and a pair of gloves to fit Sabrina. She pulled them on.

Next he went behind the counter and found the safe. He said a prayer that Gerald Nelson hadn't changed the combination in the past ten years and twisted the dial. It opened and Clay breathed a prayer of thanks. He reached for the key that would open the gun display case.

He grabbed a Sig Sauer P224 and a Glock 17 and two boxes of ammunition. "Here, can you carry this?"

She took the smaller Sig from him, loaded it and stuffed it in her coat pocket. "I don't think I can use it. I've never shot a gun before."

He lifted a brow. "It's not hard. Just point and shoot."

She shuddered. "Guns are a way of life out here and especially on your farm—I know that. But I grew up in town and never had the opportunity to learn."

He touched her cheek. "You don't have to explain. There's nothing wrong with not knowing how to use it." He frowned. "Just hold it for me in case I need it."

She nodded.

Clay took her by the hand and led her out the back and into the cold. Wind whipped her hair into her eyes and he helped her stuff it up under a black wool cap. "It's going to be a cold walk."

"I know." She squeezed his hand. "Are you going to be able to make it?"

"I have to."

Together they started through the blowing wind and snow, scarves wrapped tight, shoulders hunched. They kept to just inside the tree line. "Who do you think the boss is?" she asked as she avoided fallen logs and scattered branches.

"I don't have a clue. I haven't been back in the area long enough to figure out who's who, who has a pattern, et cetera. Ned might have some ideas."

They stopped talking for the next few minutes. Clay heard Sabrina's breathing quickening. He was grateful for the lack of dizziness and the fact the stabbing pain in his head had abated. No more shots came their way, and he silently thanked the Lord.

"There it is." She pointed.

"Finally," he breathed.

Clay picked up the pace and headed for the log cabin–type home. Sabrina stayed with him right up to the front porch, where he lifted a gloved fist to knock on the door. "Mr. Updike? You home?"

"It looks dark. Deserted."

"They have family in Florida. Probably went there for the holidays."

"Smart. I wish I had family in Florida," Sabrina muttered.

Clay knocked again.

"I'll try the back door," Sabrina said. She rushed around to the garage to find it closed. Clay joined her. "They're not here."

"We need to get inside and use the phone."

"Power's off here, too. Let's hope they have a wall phone that doesn't require electricity."

Clay went back to the front door, scanned the area.

And found what he was looking for.

He brushed the snow from the turtle nestled in the small rock garden under the bush. A silver key glinted up at him. He grabbed it and unlocked the door. Sabrina stepped into the warmth and let out a sigh. They'd made it. Now the phone.

Clay was already in the kitchen pulling the receiver from the base. He gave her a relieved look. "It's working."

She clasped her hands in front of her. "Call your parents first. Warn them about Krissy and Stan."

He dialed and waited, his tension high, head throbbing hard enough to make him nauseous. He pulled in a deep breath and closed his eyes, praying for someone to pick up the phone.

When no one answered the landline, he dialed his father's cell phone.

No answer.

Every number he dialed, no one picked up.

Clay hung up the phone as though in slow motion while his brain spun out of control. He looked at Sabrina, her fear for his family blanching her face.

His hands fisted at his sides. "We may be too late."

Urgency swept over Sabrina. Worry and more worry settled over her, and the desperate need to get to the ranch filled her. She waited while Clay dialed Ned's number. Anxiety threaded through her. "What if he doesn't answer?"

But Clay closed his eyes in relief. "Ned. I need you to send an ambulance to Nelson's Convenience

Store on Twenty-Sixth. Then I need you to get everyone out to the ranch. Krissy and Stan are behind Steven's death. They just tried to kill us." Sabrina heard Ned's roar over the line. "Lance is hurt. Bad. I'm not sure he's going to make it. But Tony saw Krissy kidnap Sabrina, so I feel sure she's headed to my parents'." He paced in front of the refrigerator. "Look, Sabrina's with me. We're on the way to the ranch. Just get help there now."

Clay hung up and checked the garage. "No car."

Defeat slammed her. "Now what?" She stood at the window. The pastures rolled with gentle snow-covered hills and the barn rose in the distance, a splash of red against the white backdrop. "I mean, I feel a thousand times better now that we've managed to get Ned involved, but I'm still worried."

"So am I." He brought a fist down on the counter. "Who else lives close by?"

Sabrina straightened. "The horses."

"What?"

"The Updikes have a lesson barn." She moved toward the door. "They have horses. Come on—I know how we're getting to your ranch."

She heard Clay follow her out the door. Her back tingled as though she had a great big bull's-eye on it. However, within seconds, they were in the barn.

With the horses and the tack they needed.

Clay caught on fast. Together they chose two horses and had them tacked up and ready to ride in record time. "Let's go. We should be there within ten minutes taking the back trails and shortcuts."

"Thank you, God, for a full moon tonight," she said.

"Amen."

Sabrina swung into the saddle. Clay did the same, but she saw him wince. He wasn't feeling as good as he was letting on. She just hoped the ride didn't hurt his head too much.

They rode hard and fast and stayed to the back trails that would lead to the Starke ranch. When Clay pulled up, Sabrina followed his lead and walked her animal up next to him. He pointed. "The ranch is just over that hill."

"How's your head?"

"That ride didn't help it, but I'll manage. How's yours?"

"Ditto."

"Ned should be there by now, but let's approach cautiously, okay? We may still have a shooter on our tails."

"Of course."

"Not only that, we're going to be out in the open for a while to get down there." He drew in a deep breath. "I don't like it."

"We don't have a choice. Let's go."

Clay reached over and grasped her hand in his. He started to say something, then snapped his lips shut and let go of her fingers. He nudged his horse into a slow walk.

Sabrina stayed beside him until they crested the hill to look down on the Starke ranch. The desolate white landscape looked peaceful and much too quiet all at the same time. "Where're Ned and the other deputies?"

He shook his head. "I don't know."

They made their way down the hill, Sabrina keenly aware of the fact that if someone wanted to start shooting, he probably wouldn't miss this time. "Something's not right, Clay. Do you think they got to Ned?"

He held his weapon in his left hand, the reigns in his right as he pulled his horse to a stop. "I'm not sure. I agree, though. Something's not right."

"I don't see anyone—do you?"

"Nothing. It's like a deserted town." He stayed put for just a moment, then nudged the horse forward. "Let's get the horses inside the fence and walk the rest of the way."

"All right." She followed him to the fence line and around to the gate. He slid to the ground and handed her his horse's reins. He opened the gate and she walked her horse through, pulling his behind her. Clay shut the gate and she dismounted. "What now?"

"Now we go find my family."

TWENTY

Clay had to admit he was scared. A ball of dread and worry sat like a rock in the pit of his belly. He knew Krissy and Stan wouldn't hesitate to kill his family if they thought it would further their cause—or keep them from going to jail.

Having Sabrina beside him made him all the more sensitive to the fact that he would have to protect her, too. He should have convinced her to stay at the store, but now he was concerned that no one had arrived to help Jordan and Lance. "Let's check the stable first." They'd left the horses in the pasture near the trees, where they could seek shelter if they wanted to. They'd be fine for now. Once he made sure his family was safe, he'd return the horses to the Updikes' barn.

Sabrina walked beside him, anxiety in every step. His gaze swept the area around them. Nothing but white. No movement, no sound. Something was very, very wrong.

At the barn, Clay stepped inside, his gun held

ready. The horses nickered at him. All seemed right enough.

Except for the movement near the last stall. Sabrina sucked in a breath. She'd seen it, too. Clay aimed his gun. "Police! Freeze!" The movement ceased. Clay darted forward. "Who's there?"

"Clay?"

Clay stopped and lowered his weapon. "Abe? What are you doing here?"

"Trying to figure out how to get the cops out here." He lifted his cell phone. "Just getting ready to call."

"Where are Mom and Dad and the rest of the family?"

"Trapped inside the house." Abe glanced in the direction of the main house. "They're going to kill them. They're just waiting on you two."

"What do you mean?" He'd never seen Abe look so pale before. Stark terror for those he loved stood clear in his eyes.

"I overheard Krissy talking on her phone. Said the plan was to wait until you two got here and they could do away with all of you at once."

"Did you happen to hear how she planned to do that?"

"A house fire," Abe said, his voice hoarse. "She told someone to bring gasoline."

Clay swallowed. How could someone deliberately plot the murder of another person? He didn't get it. Never would. "Has that someone arrived yet?"

"No, not yet. They got 'em all tied up in there."

"How did Krissy and Stan manage to get the whole family under their control?"

"Krissy held a gun to the little girl's head and said she'd blow her away if they didn't cooperate. Stan tied them up while Krissy watched their every move."

"And you couldn't get in there?"

"Nope, figured I was better off going for help. That's why I was in the barn. I needed a horse. They disabled all the vehicles."

Clay shook his head. "Then we have to figure out a way to get them out. Where are the cops? I called Ned and told him to send law enforcement out here."

"Haven't seen Ned."

Now Clay was seriously concerned. "What are they tied up with?"

"Duct tape and some rope, I think. I could see what all they used."

"Let me have your cell phone." Abe handed it over and Clay quickly punched in Ned's number. It went straight to voice mail. "Ned, where are you? I'm at the ranch and I need help. Call me ASAP." He snapped the old-fashioned phone shut. "Now he's not answering." Clay opened the phone again and called one of the other deputies, Donnie Kingston. "I need backup at the ranch and I need it now."

"Have you seen the snow, Clay? We were blessed to get home from your parents' barbecue. Roads are getting bad."

"I don't think you understand, Donnie. My family is being held hostage!" Sabrina placed a hand on his arm and he realized his voice had risen with each word. He took in a deep breath. "I don't care how you get here—just do it." He hung up and called his department in Nashville. "I know it'll take an hour for you to get here, but get a chopper in the air, something. I've got two killers in my house, and I need help now!"

His head pounded in time with his pulse. How was he going to do this? Abe's phone rang. He handed it to his uncle.

"Hello?" Abe listened. Then his eyes rose to meet Clay's. "It's for you."

"What?" Clay took the phone back. "Hello?"

"You have exactly sixty seconds to get inside this house or I start killing family members," Krissy said. She might have been ordering a pizza for all the inflection in her voice.

Clay's blood ran cold. "What do you want?"

"I just told you. Sixty seconds."

Sabrina watched Clay pace for five of those seconds. Then he stopped sharp and bolted for the tack room. When he returned, he looked at her and Abe. "Wait for backup. I've got to go in or they're going to kill someone."

"Clay—" she whispered.

He placed a hard kiss on her lips and, without another word, headed from the barn and out into the hard-falling snow.

Sabrina looked at Abe. "What are we going to do?" she demanded. "Wait for backup that may or may not be on the way?"

Abe ran a hand down his face. "That doesn't seem to be a good idea, does it?"

"He can't die, Abe." Her voice cracked, and she bit her lip. "None of them can die."

"You're right. They're not dying. Not while I have breath left in my body."

"What are you going to do?"

"I'm going to see what I can do about getting them out of there."

"How?"

"If I knew that, I'd tell you," he snapped. "Now you stay put."

"Nope. I'm going."

He stared at her. "You'll just get in the way and likely get yourself killed. Stay put."

She held his gaze. "No." Sabrina wasn't sure she wanted to work with a man who held her, at the very least, partially responsible for his bitterness, but she figured she didn't have any other options. She wasn't going to be left behind.

She saw the moment he realized he wasn't going to win this argument. He tightened his grip on his rifle and motioned her to follow him. Sabrina belatedly remembered the weapon in her jacket pocket. She slipped her hand in the pocket and curled her fingers around the grip.

Then released it. She knew she had to make a decision. Could she use the weapon or not? She pictured Krissy with her gun held to little Maria's head and felt certainty come over her.

She could do it if she had to.

"It's just the two of them. They don't have enough manpower to monitor all sides of the house. They might be glancing out the window every once in a while, but we're gonna sneak up on 'em."

Abe led Sabrina from the barn and to the side of the house. He sidled up to the window, and Sabrina held her breath. This was crazy.

Abe was crazy.

She glanced back toward the drive that would bring help. Emptiness stared back at her.

Please, Lord, bring help and bring it fast. Keep Clay and his family safe. Please don't let them die.

Clay held his hands up and focused his attention on Stan, not on the family who sat tied to various pieces of furniture in the den. He'd taken everything in with one glance when he'd walked through the kitchen door. No one had put up a fight. Krissy still held Maria by one arm, her gun never wavering from the little girl's head. Stan had Tony in much the same position. Only Stan had his sawed-off shotgun aimed in Clay's direction.

Clay pulled in a deep breath. "I'm here. Now what?"

"Where's Sabrina?" Krissy demanded. "I know she was with you."

"She was. She's safe now. You don't really think I'd let her walk into a situation like this, do you?" She frowned as though she wasn't sure whether she believed him or not. "You killed Steven." He kept his voice soft. Low. Almost soothing. It was a testament to his self-control.

Seth sat on the couch, his casted leg propped on a pillow. A fist with white knuckles lay against his thigh. He wanted to act. His parents sat in their matching recliners, hands and feet bound. White-hot rage nearly blinded him. His sister, Amber, sat on the love seat under the window, eyes narrowed and assessing, fingers clenched tight.

The pile of cell phones in the middle of the coffee table in front of her explained why he couldn't reach anyone.

Aaron lay on the floor, unconscious, a gash on his temple bleeding slightly.

"Yes," Krissy said. "But you can blame Jordan for that. He was being a tattletale."

"Who's your boss?"

Stan snorted and Krissy laughed. "You haven't figured it out yet?"

A chill swept through him. His mind clicked. The phone call. Abe's phone. Crushing despair ratcheted through him. "Yes. I think I have."

"A little late to do anything about it, though."

"So what now?"

"Now we wait on the boss to get here, and we burn down your house with everyone in it."

His mother's whimper nearly snapped his tight hold on his control. Not yet. Not yet. He flicked a glance at Seth. They'd taped only his hands together—in front of him. His crutches lay beside him next to the couch. Clay caught Seth's eyes and looked down at the crutches, then back up. Seth gave a slow nod.

Stan let Tony go, and the boy ran to Clay's mother and hugged her knees. She lifted her taped hands to rest them on his head. Stan jerked Clay's arms behind his back and used the silver duct tape to secure them. He then shoved Clay into the wing-back chair near the far wall. "Don't move. In a few minutes, the boss will be here and this will all be over soon."

The minutes ticked by.

Clay worked on his bonds while he tried to communicate with his eyes. Stan no longer held Tony hostage, but any wrong move might spur Krissy into pulling the trigger on Maria.

Krissy and Stan didn't speak. Stan paced, and Krissy twitched, her nerves ready to get the best of her. Clay cleared his throat. "While we're waiting on your boss, will you please tell me why you had to kill Steven?"

She looked almost relieved at his question. "Trey called and said Jordan had pictures of me and my customers at the meth lab on his camera and that he'd given some hard copies to Steven. I couldn't take a chance he would figure out who was in those pictures."

"So you had Trey set him up and you killed him. And Trey." Rage ripped through him, and he had to concentrate on keeping his cool, staying calm. Going ballistic wouldn't help the situation.

"It's the way things work sometimes."

"No, not for sane people," Clay retorted.

Krissy's eyes flashed. "Jordan had been snooping around. One of my customers saw him and went ballistic. Jordan ran, but I knew who he was. I had to get him and his stupid camera. But he was pretty quick and sneaky. I ran into him in town and when he didn't react to seeing me, I realized he didn't know who I was, that I must not have been in his pictures. I know now I was, but I was a blur.

So the fact that he didn't know I was involved in the meth ring made things a little easier."

"Easier to set him up to kill him?"

She snickered. "Yeah. Exactly."

"But then he found Steven's wallet in Stan's trailer."

Krissy's pleased expression sobered and she shot a look at Stan. "Apparently."

"How did it get there, Krissy?" Clay asked, keeping his voice soft. "Did you plant it there hoping Stan would take the fall for Steven's death?"

"Murder," his father stated. "Call it what it is."

Krissy's gaze swung to Clay's father. Clay caught the man's eye and gave a slight shake of his head. "Come on, Krissy, you were trying to set Stan up. With Sabrina dead, the authorities would swarm the place, find the wallet in Stan's trailer, and Stan would take the fall for everything." He blinked. "No, that's not the way it was supposed to go down. You couldn't let Stan take the rap. He had to be dead, too, didn't he? Because he could identify you. You were going to kill them all, weren't you?"

Krissy's mouth worked and Stan's jaw hung, his face turning a different shade of red with each word Clay uttered. Clay pushed the point. "Yes, I think I have it figured out now. You told Jordan to lure Sabrina to Stan's trailer. You planned to kill her and Jordan. Then you were going to lie in wait for Stan to come home and kill him, probably making it look like a suicide."

Krissy's face whitened and she took a step back.

"I knew it!" Stan roared. "You said the kid had the wallet all along, but you were setting me up!"

"Stop it, Stan. Think about what Clay's saying. What he's doing. He's trying to get us to turn on each other. So just settle down." She looked back at Clay. "Now I think it's time for you to shut up."

"Just one more question."

"What?"

"Why?"

Krissy frowned. "Why what?"

"Why choose this life? You have a husband who loves you, people in town who think you're a great teacher and respect you. Why throw it all away?"

She stiffened. Maria wiggled, and Krissy jerked her back. "Be still, brat."

"Let me go! You're mean!"

Krissy ignored her and looked at Clay. "I'm not throwing it all away. I'm simply tying up some loose ends to ensure no one finds out." She sneered. "I hate this dead-end town. I want out."

"They why not just leave?" Seth asked her. Krissy stood next to the sofa now. In her rant, she'd tried to pace. Keeping Maria with her had hindered her progress a bit, but Clay was satisfied with her location. He raised a brow at Seth, who nodded and shifted.

"And go where?" Krissy shouted. "And do what with no money? Why? You want to know why? So I *could* leave. Leave it all behind. My sick mother, my suck-up brother and my lame husband."

The door slammed open, and Clay flinched. He twisted so he could see. Sabrina stepped through first, hands held high, followed by Abe in the same posture. Behind them, rifle held centered on Abe's back, came the boss.

Clay's jaw tightened. He forced it to relax. "Hello, Ned."

TWENTY-ONE

A collective gasp came from the rest of his family as they put it together. "Why, Ned?" His father's agonized question hung in the air as Ned gestured to Stan to set about duct-taping Sabrina's and Abe's hands and legs.

Abe gave Stan a shove and pulled back his fist.

"Stop!" Krissy's shriek pierced the air. "I'll shoot her!"

Clay swung his attention to Krissy, who had the gun pressed against little Maria's temple. Maria didn't look scared, just furious, her big blue eyes shooting sparks at the woman who kept her captive.

Abe dropped his arm. Stan swung the shotgun and caught Abe on the chin. Clay winced as his uncle stumbled back and hit the wall. Next Stan pointed the weapon at Clay.

"No!" Sabrina launched herself at Stan, and the two of them tumbled to the floor, the shotgun skidding. Stan pushed Sabrina away and grabbed the weapon. This time he pointed it at her.

"Move and I'll fill you full of holes."

"No holes, Stan. It has to look like an accident," Krissy said. He prodded Sabrina in the back, and she moved to sit on the floor beside Clay. Stan had her hands bound in front of her within seconds.

Clay eyed the gas can Ned set on the floor. "Arson investigators are pretty good these days."

"Yes, well, we all know who will help in the investigation. I think we'll be fine."

Clay didn't take his eyes from Ned's. "Why?"

"Money." For a moment shame stood out clearly on the man's face. He quickly covered. "Money. The diner is going under. We all know how well my job pays." He snorted. "And I got a kid with a drug problem."

"Lily?" Sabrina gasped.

"Yes. Prescription drugs." He shook his head, his grief visible. "That car accident has nearly destroyed our family. It was Lily's fault and the other person sued. I had to take another loan out against the diner and my house to help her. And with the economy in the tank, I'm about to lose everything." Clay thought he saw tears in his eyes for a moment. Then they were gone. "You got to do what you got to do to protect your family."

"Yes," Clay said. "You sure do."

They sat on the floor against the wall. Sabrina's gaze met Clay's.

Ned handed the gasoline can to Stan. "Get it

good. There's more where that came from." Stan walked outside. The sheriff looked at Clay's father. "I never meant for Steven to get killed. Krissy did it, and I didn't find out about it until later. Once I realized everything that happened, I couldn't arrest her."

"Because she would turn you in."

"Exactly."

Sabrina struggled to get her taped hands into her pocket without attracting Krissy's or Ned's attention. Finally, she managed to get her fingers wrapped around the grip. Slowly, her eyes swiveling between Stan and Krissy, heart pounding, expecting to be caught at any moment, she pulled the weapon from her pocket.

Stan had taped Clay's hands behind his back, but she could see he'd worked them free. Low on the floor, she lifted the gun and nudged Clay's free right hand. He didn't look at her, just wrapped his fingers around the barrel and kept it behind him.

She didn't know what he could do with it, but surely it would be something. Fear trembled through her. Prayers winged from her lips. Tony stared at her. Maria sobbed her anger. Fear morphed into fury, and Sabrina brought her knees up. She buried her face in her hands, hoping it looked as if she had just given up. She sank her teeth into the duct tape.

"Now," she heard Clay say.

She snapped her head up in time to see Seth swing one of his crutches up from beside the couch and catch Krissy's arm. The gun tumbled from her hand and hit the floor. She screamed and froze as Seth grabbed it and brought it up to center it on her face.

Clay moved at the same time, bringing the Sig Sauer around to level it on Ned, who stood frozen with his rifle aimed at Clay. "Drop it, Ned."

"I can't," the man whispered.

A shadow moved behind Ned, and the muzzle of a small pistol settled at the base of his skull. "But I can and I will if you don't drop your gun." Ned's shoulders wilted and Sabrina could see he realized he was done.

Jordan bolted around the sheriff, still holding his weapon on him.

"Jordan!" Maria cried out and raced over to wrap her arms around his legs. Clay removed the rifle from Ned's hands as law enforcement swarmed into the house.

Krissy screamed and made a break for the back of the house. Sabrina pushed her legs out straight and caught her in the shins, and the woman went down with a thud.

Seth held Krissy's weapon above his head as another officer grabbed her and cuffed her. She felt Clay tugging at the duct tape on her hands and then they were free. He pulled her up and wrapped his arms around her.

"Hey, what about the rest of us?" Abe grunted. Clay gave her a quick kiss and started freeing his family.

Sabrina went to Jordan. "I'm so glad you're okay." Maria and Tony had latched themselves on to their big brother and weren't letting go anytime soon. "Did Lance get help?"

Jordan nodded. "They airlifted him to a hospital in Nashville. I hitched a ride with the cops and brought them here. They said they knew Clay."

Sabrina nodded. Clay walked up beside her. She gripped his hand and gave it a squeeze. "How did you know it was Ned?"

"The phone call in the barn. I used Abe's phone to call Ned. Krissy called me on that number. She had no idea what Abe's number was. Ned had to have given it to her. I just didn't think fast enough."

"You'd already called for backup, so I guess it didn't really matter."

"No. I still would have done exactly the same thing."

Officers led Krissy and Ned toward the door. Clay broke away from her to hug his parents and tell Seth, "Nice work, bro."

"Just like when we were kids sneaking something past Mom and Dad."

"I was hoping you'd remember."

Seth gave a small grin. "Like I could ever forget." His expression turned serious. "I'm just glad I didn't miss."

"You? Miss? Not likely. I also remember how well you could swing a bat."

"Hey, now, that was an accident."

Clay rubbed the back of his head as Sabrina's gaze bounced between the two of them. "Right."

Ross Starke held his wife close to him as she sobbed on his shoulder. "You two can joke about this?"

Clay sobered. "No, Dad. Not joking. Just relieved everyone survived what could have been a nightmare situation."

"Your brother didn't survive."

Clay dropped his head. "No. No, he didn't."

Sabrina cleared her throat. "I'm sorry to interrupt, but I know Mrs. Starke and Daisy Ann are friends." She looked at the woman, who continued to dry her tears on a mangled tissue. "Do you think you could be the one to tell her about Ned? She's going to be devastated and I think if you were there with her, it would help her tremendously. Maybe reassure her that you don't hold her husband's actions against her."

Mrs. Starke swallowed and drew in a shuddering breath. "I…I don't know." But the tears had stopped. Sabrina hoped she would start thinking about something she could do, be proactive and stop feeling like a victim. Her shoulders straightened. "Yes. I'll tell her. Ross, will you take me?"

Ross frowned. "But what about—"

"I've got it covered, Dad." Clay shot Sabrina a look full of gratitude, and she gave a relieved sigh that she'd spoken up.

Amber stepped up beside them. "Dad and I'll take you, Mom. Lily might need me to be there for her, too."

Sabrina took Clay's hand. "Just curious, how did you get that tape off so fast while your hands were behind your back?"

"In the barn, when Abe said they used duct tape and rope, I simply got a razor blade from the tack room and stuck it in my back pocket. As soon as Stan taped me up, I got the blade and started working." He gave her a squeeze. "I'm glad you noticed my hands were free and were able to slip me the gun."

Abe placed a hand on her shoulder. She flinched and leaned into Clay. Abe dropped his hand with a look of shame. "Sorry."

Sabrina straightened. "No, it's okay. I'm sorry."

"You tried to defend me."

"Oh. Yes. Well…"

"Thank you."

She smiled. "Of course." She looked at the bruise forming on his chin. "I'm afraid I didn't do a very good job, though."

Abe rubbed the wounded spot. "In this case, we'll go with 'It's the thought that counts.'" He started to turn, stopped and spun back around. "By the way, you two have my blessing. Not that you need or want it, but you have it." And then he was gone.

Clay slipped an arm around Sabrina's shoulders. "Speaking of blessings…I'm ready to count mine."

EPILOGUE

Christmas Eve day

Sabrina swept the last of the leaves from the porch of the bed-and-breakfast and smiled when Clay's police cruiser pulled into the parking lot. She leaned on the broom and waited for him to open the door. It had been three weeks since all the excitement at the farm. It felt like three years in some ways, three days in others. "Merry Christmas."

He grinned and bounded up the stairs to plant a warm greeting on her lips. "Merry Christmas."

"What brings you by?"

"You, of course." He glanced at the door behind her. "How's Granny May?"

"Doing much better. She just finished baking her famous apple pie."

Clay licked his lips and she laughed. Then sobered. "How's Lance doing?" She knew he'd been by to see his friend, who was now home and recovering from the gunshot wound.

"Daisy Ann's taking care of him."

"I think it's good for her to have him to focus on. Have you talked to Ned?"

"I tried. He refuses to see me."

"I'm so sorry." She tilted her head and looked up at him. "I talked to Lily yesterday. She's in rehab and wants me to come see her soon. She's heart-broken over her father."

"She didn't have a clue, did she?"

"No." Sabrina felt that familiar stab of sorrow dart through her. She forced it away, refusing to allow dark memories to ruin her time with Clay. "You want to come in?"

"No, can we take a walk around back?"

"Sure." She leaned the broom against the rail of the porch and took his proffered hand. "What's going on?"

They walked out to the small gazebo Sabrina had decorated with greenery and mistletoe. They settled on the bench and Sabrina fired up the gas logs in the middle.

Clay wrapped an arm around her shoulders and she snuggled into his side. "We've spent a lot of time in this little spot over the last several weeks, haven't we?"

"A lot." They'd sat and talked into the wee hours of the night, just enjoying each other's company and getting to know one another, sharing fears and dreams. Sabrina had never felt closer to another person in her life.

He cleared his throat. "You know how you told me last week that if the opportunity presented itself, you would want to know about your mother?"

She stilled. "Yes."

"Do you still feel that way?"

Sabrina pulled in a deep breath. "You know something?"

"I found her."

"Is she alive?"

"No. She's buried in Nashville, where she'd been living from the time she left you to the time she died."

"When did she die?" Curiously, Sabrina felt no grief, just a gut-clenching sadness that her mother had never known true happiness or peace.

"Twelve years ago. She was living under another name and had no relatives listed when she died."

"How did she die?"

"Breast cancer."

"Oh." She paused and let it sink in. She hadn't expected that. She'd thought he would say she'd died from a drug overdose or something similar. Sabrina felt a sense of closure wash over her. "Thank you."

"Sure. She kept her same Social Security number, just changed her name. That's how I was able to track her. She married a guy by the name of Harold Jeeves. Seemed like a nice fellow. He stayed with her the whole time and said she'd changed a lot before she died."

"But she never contacted me."

"I asked him about that. He said they came to Wrangler's Corner one day after she was diagnosed fifteen years ago, but they saw you and your grandmother shopping and you seemed so happy. Your mother decided to let you live your life without disrupting it with her return."

"Oh." Sabrina wasn't sure what to think about that but maybe her mother had found some peace after all.

"Are you okay?"

She nodded. "Yes. I'm okay. Sad, but okay."

"All right, now I have a question for you."

She stilled. "Okay."

"Well, first I need to tell you something."

He sounded so nervous. Which set off her nerves. She slid away from him a little so she could look into his eyes. "What is it, Clay?"

He swallowed. "I was offered the sheriff's position here in Wrangler's Corner."

"Really?"

"Yes. Lance turned it down, so I'm second choice." His lips twisted in a small smile.

She hugged his arm and kissed him. "You're first choice in my book." She sighed and dropped her gaze. "I'll never be able to say that word without thinking of Steven."

He hugged her back. "I know. I feel the same way. But I think Steven would approve of everything we've done to bring his killers to justice."

She smiled up at him. "I do, too."

"You know what else I think he would approve of?"

"What?"

He kissed her cheeks, then her nose, then her lips. "Us."

"Mmm…I approve of that, too." She frowned. "So you plan to take the sheriff's job? What about your job in Nashville? You just made detective."

"You're not in Nashville."

Sabrina swallowed. Hard. "No. I'm not."

"Your grandmother needs you right now, and I know how important she is to you. She's important to me, too. My family is going through some issues, too. I think I need to stay here and do what I can to help. Aaron and Amber are doing their thing and Seth is sullen, hurting and trying to heal." He blew out a breath. "I want to be here for them."

"What about later?"

"Later?"

"When they don't need you anymore. Will you feel stuck here in Wrangler's Corner?"

"Stuck? No. Honestly? When I was in Nashville, I was doing good work. I was happy. At least I thought I was."

"But?"

"But…" he flushed "…I missed home." He shook his head. "I'm glad I've done what I've done, but being here the last four weeks has really shown me where I belong."

"In Wrangler's Corner."

"Yes, but mostly? With you."

"I'm glad, Clay."

"I know it hasn't been long, but I'm in love with you, Sabrina, and I know for a fact that no matter how long we know each other, how long we date, that's not going to change." He paused. "Except maybe to grow stronger."

Sabrina threw her arms around his neck and kissed him through her tears. "I'm so thankful God brought you home. Not that Steven had to die—I don't think we'll ever understand why that had to happen—but I think Steven would be proud of you. He'd be pleased and get a big laugh out of the fact that his death brought us together."

Clay drew her into a tight hug. "I don't want to wait forever to marry you, Sabrina. I understand if you need some time, but—"

"But what?"

He cleared his throat, set her back from him and slid to the ground to face her. She caught her breath. Goose bumps popped out and she felt the butterflies burst free in her midsection.

He lifted one hand and kissed her knuckles. "Will you do me the honor of being my wife?"

"I love you, Clay."

"Is that a yes?"

She laughed as he wiped the tears from her cheeks. "It's definitely a yes. How about an Easter wedding?"

He grinned. "I approve of that."

* * * * *

Dear Reader,

I wrote the beginning of this story several times before I was happy with it. After writing sixteen books for Love Inspired Suspense, I thought I had it down. Not this time. Although I want each story to be perfect. that isn't exactly a realistic goal, although I do believe it's admirable and something to shoot for. However, I've come to the realization that perfection isn't possible and I'm okay with that. Sabrina also had to come to peace with this fact. She couldn't see past her mother's imperfections to the fact that she had a grandmother who loved her unconditionally until the hero pointed it out to her.

I'm so thankful that I have a Savior who loves me, who died for me, so that I don't have to worry about being perfect. I can just do my best to live as He's called me to do. I pray if you're struggling with the need to be perfect, you will allow Him to take your imperfections and turn them into things that bring joy, glory and honor to Him.

God bless,
Lynette

Questions for Discussion

1. Both the heroine and hero had interesting pasts. How do you think their pasts made them into the people they were when the story opened?

2. What did you think about the heroine's desire to save the kids no matter the danger to her own life? Do you feel that way about anyone in your life? Why or why not?

3. What did you think about Abe Starke? How had his bitterness affected his relationships with his family?

4. What did you think about Ross Starke, Clay's father, telling his brother to get off his land at the cost of possibly losing the ranch? Do you think he did the right thing? Why or why not?

5. Who was your favorite character in the story?

6. Was there a character you could identify with in the story? If so, who was it and why did you identify with that person?

7. What was your favorite scene?

8. Sabrina was determined not to be left behind. Do you think it was a wise decision for her to go with Clay to confront the killers?

9. What did you think about Abe's conversion in the end? Should it have taken Sabrina putting her life on the line for him in order for him to find forgiveness in his heart? Or do you think God can use those kinds of things to bring us around?

10. In the end, everything worked out. Were you surprised when you found out who the villain was? Do you think circumstances can force someone to do something he never would have considered before hard times hit?

11. In response to the previous question, I believe that's one reason to hang on to God, to have an active, ongoing relationship with Him. That way, when the bad times come, and they will, there's no question about what to do or where to place your faith. Do you agree? Disagree? Why?